Xtabentum: A Novel of Yucatan

By
Rosy Hugener with Carl Hugener

This book was published by Rosa Hugener with Carl Hugener
SHARED PEN Edition
www.SharedPen.com
For information about the book go to
www.Xtabentum.com

To my family: Carl, Joseph, Ana, Buelis, Papi, Tita, Meche, Ivonne, Bony, Pao, Dany y Mechita.

This book is a work of fiction. While actual historical figures appear and certain historical events are described, the authors' primary objective is not historical accuracy. We have not consciously changed any events, but have changed timing slightly to accommodate the story. The words and ideas of all characters are products of our imagination

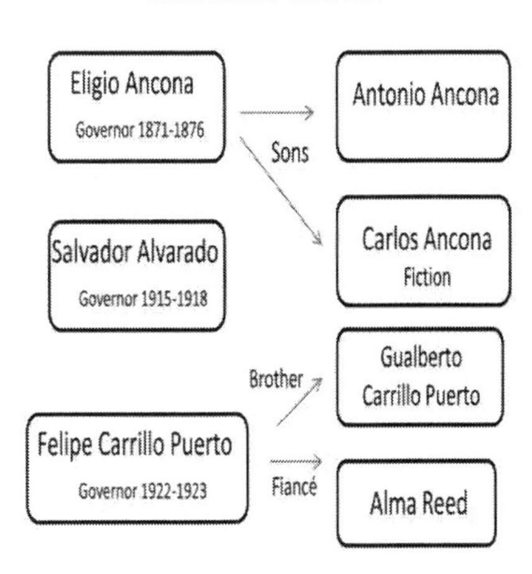
Real Historical Characters
Eligio Ancona
Governor 1871-1876
Antonio Ancona
Sons
Salvador Alvarado
Governor 1915-1918
Carlos Ancona
Fiction
Brother
Gualberto
Carrillo Puerto
Felipe Carrillo Puerto
Governor 1922-1923
Fiancé
Alma Reed

Table of Contents

Prologue 5
Merida, Yucatan, 1906 5
Chapter One: Dziú's Son 7
Mexico City, 1985 7
Chapter 2: Xtabentum 15
Merida, 1915 15
Chapter 3: Peregrina (The Pilgrim) 25
Merida, 1922 25
Chapter 4: The Magician's Pyramid (Uxmal) 35
Merida, 1922 35
Chapter 5: Xtabey 44
Merida, 1922 44
Chapter 6: The Way to Xibalba 57
Merida, 1923 57
Chapter 7:Huevos Motuleños (Motul-style Eggs) 70
Merida, 1923 70
Chapter 8: Cenotes 88
Merida, 1985-1986 88
Chapter 9: The Lost Jacket 117
Merida, 1924 117
Chapter 10: Henequen 131
Chicago, 1924 131
Chapter 11: The Final Truth 166
Mexico City, 1986 166

Prologue

Merida, Yucatan, 1906

The night in Merida was so hot and humid that all the houses had extinguished their lights, trying to avoid even that much extra heat. Only one house was awake, filled with anxious movements. A beautiful woman writhed on a bed, screaming. She was having a baby, her face reflecting uncontrolled pain as sweat ran down her forehead. But her eyes were paralyzed, fixed on a window, expressionless. A sudden thunderclap broke the night and shocked the woman back to reality, but the empty look soon returned. From her window, it was possible to see lightning, flashes of light like the sun reflecting on machetes. The lightning flashes just made her sadder. They just made her remember.

A few moments later, as the baby screamed her entrance into the world, a dense fog invaded the room, only to retreat as suddenly as it had arrived, hiding under the bed sheets and in the tile cracks, from where it would haunt the room forever.

Shortly after that, the baby found two warm and ready hands to cuddle. The difference of skin color was quite noticeable when the baby found the woman's breast. And with her nurse's milk, Amanda found the cinnamon love that would inhabit her body for the rest of her life.

Chapter One: Dziú's Son

Mexico City, 1985

•

Chac, the rain god, noticed dry and under-nourished plants struggling to live in the weak soil of the Earth. He decided to burn the land to increase nutrients in the soil. Chac called on all birds to help him. He asked them to save all plant seeds, especially seeds of the corn that was so helpful to men.

The fire started, and all birds did their work picking up the closest seeds they found. One particularly colorful bird with brown eyes searched desperately for cornfields, but the smoke was thick and it was almost impossible to see. At last, the colorful bird found the corn. Without regard for the fire and his own safety, he swooped in to save the seeds. Unfortunately, the bird was disfigured by the fire, and lost his beauty. His eyes were turned to red.

Chac wanted to reward this hero of a bird, so the rest of the birds were told that from this time on, the hero would not need to nest or care for its young. Other birds would be foster parents. This red-eyed bird was called Dziu.

- Mayan Legend

There are profound events that shape our lives, and there are small moments that change the way we see life. I was about to experience one of those moments, and it would bring me to see how events decades before had shaped my family. A life founded on lies creates a whirlwind of false memories, straining to escape its bottle. When it escapes, will it tear our lives apart, or pass us by, giving us only the gentle touch of an afternoon breeze?

I had moved to Chicago ten years earlier, and since then I had had many happy visits to Mexico. But this time I was flying back to Mexico City to visit my grandmother for the last time. She had been suffering from Alzheimer's disease for several years, and her health had recently become much worse. She was holding onto life with her last bit of energy, and my family told me that she was often barely conscious.

I left my husband and children behind at O'Hare and boarded a crowded plane full of Mexican-Americans whose faces held the longing look of those ready to set foot once again in their homeland. They were mostly emigrants like me, people who had filled their bags with presents and dressed themselves in their best clothes for their reunions with cherished family. Teenagers proudly wore Chicago Cubs jackets or Bulls t-shirts. A mixture of Spanish and English flowed between the family members.

After a smooth landing, I went through immigration, picked up my bags, cleared customs, and faced an avalanche, both of people and emotions, when the exit doors opened to the airport terminal.

Outside the doors of the customs area was a raucous crowd of hundreds waiting for loved ones. I saw watery eyes of people holding large bouquets of flowers, and a hand-painted banner welcoming someone named Javier. Children tried to sneak past the security guards, who caught them and sent them back to their clustered groups of relatives and friends. A wave of shouts rose every time the doors opened to reveal another passenger. In the midst of the crowd, I focused on a familiar smile, and there was my father with one hand up high, trying to attract my attention. I rushed over to him and, in his embrace, smelled the cologne that made me feel at home.

After hurrying through the terminal to the parking garage, I snatched my father's car keys from his hands, eager to experience once again the excitement of driving in Mexico City. As had been the case in each of my visits for the past ten years, there was road construction in the area of the airport terminals, but soon enough, we reached the highway. I drove like a kamikaze. I had my six senses tuned to the road; in Mexico City, you need the extra one. It felt wonderful to drive without worrying about speed limits, police with radar guns, and distracted drivers using cruise control. It was a jungle, but my kind of jungle.

The lanes were so narrow and the cars so close together that I could hardly believe I was navigating them, not to mention doing so at a great speed. As we neared the Las Lomas exit, we hit "the wall," as my father liked to call that point on the highway where traffic was always backed up, no matter what the hour. Some things never changed. The traffic in Mexico City is like a baby who never grows up, alternating without warning between great joy and great sorrow. One car was using an entrance ramp as an exit, backing up for hundreds of yards, and another was jumping the curb. This is how people drive in Mexico City.

At last, we arrived in the neighborhood where I had grown up. I smiled as we drove down streets that had the same potholes and unpainted speed bumps that I had memorized throughout my life. We drove past the Catholic elementary school I had attended. It surprised me to see that there were now iron bars on the windows. I guessed the nuns were worried that some of their prisoners might escape. A little girl crossing the street with her blue and red uniform took me back to a time when having a skirt a little too short was the worst sin in the world.

We finally drove onto my street. I imagined my various neighbors in their windows greeting me: the staunch religious family with eight children; the little girl who had lost two fingers when a flowerpot fell and crushed them; the family who hated mine because of a rivalry over a boyfriend; the family from Monterrey who owned furniture stores; the Spanish sculptor with the two floor-to-ceiling windows in his studio.

The ghosts were waving at me with white silk neckerchiefs, as in a bullring when the crowd wants to save the bull. I could see them clearly, even though they were all off living their own lives.

I arrived at my family's house and rushed to my grandmother's room. She was laying quietly on her bed with her eyes closed. Her slim body looked smaller than I remembered, her skin was almost transparent, and her nails looked like they would break with the smallest touch. There was a smile on her face.

I called her name several times but she did not answer. Before the Alzheimer's disease, she had hearing problems, so I shouted as loudly as I could. She finally opened her eyes. She looked at me and it made me feel the same way as when I looked into the eyes of my children when they were very young. I saw innocence and happiness. She was waiting for me to do something. She had that impatient look that was telling me, "Come on, do something, anything." I shouted a couple of nonsensical words. She looked back at me and repeated exactly the same words that I said, ending them with a broad smile.

I said, "I love you."

She said, "I love you."

This was our goodbye, and I knew that I would treasure it for the rest of my life.

I stayed with her for several more hours having a bizarre, repetitive conversation, but she said nothing more that was coherent. She died quietly the next morning, as if she had simply forgotten how to breathe.

The next days were a black cloud to me. My father, my aunt, my two sisters and I went through the endless ceremonies and visits from friends and loved-ones, but mostly I kept to myself and thought about my grandmother, who had raised me after my mother had died as a complication of my birth. How could I say goodbye to someone so important to me, who had stepped forward and sacrificed so much of her own life to make mine better? The memories I had of my grandmother during those days after her death continue to come back to me, as a random word or smell can trigger a flood of memory and emotion.

At the end of the week, the immediate family was back together in my grandmother's bedroom to help with the final cleaning. My aunt wanted to keep the room as my grandmother had left it.

Then Mercedes, the oldest of the three sisters, noticed the set of keys on the bedside table.

These keys were special. They were all together in a pouch that my grandmother always kept hidden inside her bra, walking around all day long with them, only putting them down on the nightstand when she was ready to sleep. These were the keys to her closet -- the big closet that held the most important things in the world: chocolates, forbidden toys and we knew not what more. Dreams?

As children, my sisters and I made many plans and many attempts to steal those keys. We never did it right. We tried sneaking into the room in the middle of the night, only to realize that we had the keys but could not open the closet without making so much noise that we would wake her up.

We even tried once or twice while she was showering. She had a large bathroom, and her habit was to leave the keys on the sink. Unfortunately, the noise of opening the bathroom door made my grandmother scream and we would have to make up stupid explanations for the intrusion.

Now Mercedes asked, "Can we open the closet?" She said it with a sly smile.

We all agreed instantly, and gave the honor to my father, joking that he likely had the most toys in there. The closet was always the place for the toy that had been taken away as punishment.

The closet was about nine feet wide and eight feet high, with doors of solid mahogany. The lock was an old-looking, bronze, tubular relic. The door slid open with a groan to reveal my grandmother's life.

We took turns emptying out the contents. My aunt first found an envelope with everyone's school records, those of my father, my aunt, my two sisters and me. We laughed to see my father's grades because he had always bragged about them, but in fact they were worse than ours were. Looking at the school pictures, we concluded that I had the "beautiful" wide nose of my father, while my middle sister Ivonne had the bulbous nose of my aunt.

"We are going to have their noses when we grow up," I said, as if we were not already adults with bad noses.

My aunt opened a medium-sized jewelry box. Alongside the jewelry my grandmother always used for special occasions, we found two or three dozen unpaired earrings, mostly gold and silver, plus some cheap pairs from street fairs. I recognized a pearl earring that I used for years when I was a girl.

My grandmother had her favorite dresses hanging on the left side, and while we were looking through them, I remembered her at parties, with her short, bright hair that stood out and brought admiration of its fullness and whiteness.

We went through all her things little by little. She had 25 bottles of Shalimar perfume -- that is the problem with letting people know your favorite fragrance -- and 3 half-empty bottles of Lourdes water. We found an old doll in a box that Mercedes claimed as hers.

We were about to finish when at the back of the closet we found a wooden box about the size of two shoeboxes. It was surprisingly heavy, and when we opened it, we found it filled with silver coins.

"We found the treasure!" We all laughed.

We struggled to lift the heavy box out of the closet. The coins were almost black and in need of cleaning, but we all thanked my grandmother for not disappointing us.

After sorting everything and disposing of obvious trash, we decided to put the contents back into the closet as they had been. I lifted the heavy box and while I was trying to move it, it slipped from my hands and collided with the back of the closet with a loud bump. Something strange happened. A small section of loose paneling pulled away from the wall, revealing two yellowed papers.

"This is even better than treasure!" I exclaimed.

I removed the papers very carefully and held them high as if my team had just won the World Cup and I was hoisting the trophy. My family clapped, then began crowding around me to try to see what I had in my hands.

The first page was a photograph of my young grandmother with her sister and two men whom none of us recognized. She looked very happy leaning on a tree trunk, and she was looking at someone or something that was out-of-frame to her right. Ivonne pointed out that there was the shadow of someone's hands in that part of the photo, as if they had just run out of the picture frame at the last moment. On the back of the photograph, there were just two words written in a small print: "Love, Alma."

The second page looked like an official document in English. I read it, and to my surprise, I found that it was the birth certificate of a baby named Antonio, like my father, but with different middle and last names. The birth date of this child was four months before the day we had always celebrated as my father's birthday.

We were all in shock. My father grasped the paper and confirmed that my grandmother, Amanda Diaz, was listed as the mother and that the father was unknown. This child had been born in Chicago, and his name was Antonio Villanueva Diaz.

This was the moment that began my days of research. The quest to uncover the mystery of my father's birth would change our lives. It entranced and humbled us, and the outcome would haunt me. Events of decades earlier affected us as if they had happened yesterday.

Chapter 2: Xtabentum

Merida, 1915

• •

In a small Mayan town in Yucatan there lived two women. One, Xkeban, was scorned by the townspeople because of her passion for men. The other, Utz-Colel, was a beautiful, modest woman, well-accepted by others, and had never had a love affair.

But Xkeban had a big heart. She gave away expensive clothing and jewelry to save sick people or help the poor. Utz-Colel was cold-hearted, never helped the sick and felt disgusted by the poor.

The townspeople began to notice a long absence of Xkeban. Thinking that she was pursuing a love affair in a far-off town, they did not pay much attention until one day the strange aroma of a sweet flower surrounded the town. Before long, they realized that the smell came from Xkeban's house, and discovered her alone in death. The townspeople buried her, and the next day a bed of beautiful, aromatic wildflowers covered her grave.

This humble and beautiful little flower is called Xtabentum, and grows wild all around Yucatan. Its exquisite liquor extract is said to get men drunk with sweet love.

A short time later, Utz-Colel died as well. But the aroma coming from her body was the putrid smell of death.

- Mayan Legend

Nine-year-old Amanda was a girl with light brown hair, large hazel eyes and freckles on her nose. She had a refined look and the soft expression of dreamy eyes.

Early one morning, Amanda was happy, excited to start a new day while everyone else was still asleep. She ran out of her bedroom to the middle of the courtyard at the center of the house. As she stood there, she felt exactly as a king does when surveying his empire.

Amanda's house occupied an entire block in the city of Merida, and was conveniently located just two blocks from the Plaza Mayor, the center and main district of the city. Ironically, the plaza had a small park in front called "The Mothers' Park," a constant painful reminder to Amanda of the lack of her mother's companionship. The house was in the typical Spanish-Mexican style, with hallways around the courtyard leading to all the rooms.

Amanda looked around. To her left were the living room and the dining room, while to her right were her parents' bedroom with their sitting room, followed by her sister's room and her own. A big wooden door connected the main courtyard with another patio, which housed the service area: utility rooms, the kitchen, laundry, servants' quarters, and horse stables, followed by a big garden.

As Amanda entered the courtyard, she was just in time to meet Cacho, her best friend. Cacho's real name was Carmen, but everyone called her by her nickname, which meant "a little piece of life," and came from her being so short. Cacho and Amanda met daily at the pointed blue diamond that came from the morning sun shining through the blue lead windows of the main hall. They would not start talking to each other until their feet looked blue. It had become a superstitious game that would determine how well or how badly the day would go.

Cacho waited for her with a big smile on her face. She had long black hair, braided in two plaits and tied around her head. Her eyes were as dark as those of a Yucatan black jaguar. Cacho was the daughter of Jovita, Amanda's wet nurse, and was born just two months before Amanda. The two girls had shared their lives for as long as they could remember.

They had a lot to plan. Gracielita was coming to play that day, and they were planning a prank. The last time Gracielita had visited Amanda, she had refused to play with Cacho because she was a servant's daughter, making Cacho feel bad about herself. Today Amanda and Cacho would have revenge.

They had planned the prank for days. One of the family's dogs had fleas. Normally, the observant servants would spot this and the poor animal would be cleaned and shaven, but this week had been very busy. There was a new neighbor moving next door – the Peon widow – and the Diaz family was organizing a welcome party. It would be very easy while everyone was busy with the party for Amanda and Cacho to sneak off and use Gracielita's comb on the dog, and then, good-bye blond curls.

Amanda and Cacho talked and laughed for few minutes until Cacho left to do her chores.

The next-door neighbor's relocation was important news. Rosaura Peon had lost her husband one month before. He had died suddenly of a heart attack, scared to death, and she was moving back to the city with serious resentments and ready to strike back at the world in some way.

The Peon family was an important owner of a group of henequen haciendas. The beautiful spiked henequen plant produced a rich fiber that was the strongest available for decades and widely sought after for making rope and twine.

It was the leading export of the Yucatan peninsula at the beginning of the century, and the source of the region's wealth.

The new Mexican government was trying to fix the price of henequen to break apart the American henequen monopoly and open the market to other buyers, but they encountered a great deal of resistance from the old hacienda families like the Peons, who were reluctant to change a system that had made them so wealthy.

Some hacienda owners were visited by unofficial government gunmen in an effort to keep the henequen price fixed. They used very persuasive methods of intimidation to make the owners agree.

These unofficial bandidos broke into the Peon hacienda one day. They did not get the signature they wanted, and they did not use their guns either. Mr. Peon died of a heart attack with his chair facing the door of his study. And so, Mrs. Peon left the business to her brother and moved to Merida, next door to Amanda's house.

Amanda, back in the middle of the patio, scurried over and began to climb the beautiful mature laurel tree that stood in the middle of the courtyard like a tower, facing her mother's rooms. Soon she saw her coming out of her bedroom.

Norma, Amanda's mother, was wearing a white traditional peasant's dress called a hipil, with cross-stitched embroidered roses along the neckline. This loose, rectangular, semi-transparent outfit dimly revealed her naked body beneath. She was so pale that she looked like a ghost, or the soft shadow left in one's eyes after looking at the sun.

Norma could not see Amanda because a curtain of leaves hid her. Neither did Amanda see her mother completely – the tree was filtering the image like patches of reality, like stars of happiness. Norma opened one of the birdhouses hanging around the hall and with her soft, delicate hands took out a yellow canary. She gently rubbed her right cheek on the soft feathers that were more white than yellow. As she turned toward the tree, she looked directly at the spot where Amanda sat. Norma could not see her, but Amanda imagined that the gentle love in her mother's eyes was directed at her, and for a moment, she touched happiness. It was going to be a great day.

Norma went back to her room and Amanda was just coming down from the tree when Jovita walked into the patio. The entire house was coming alive and the servants were emerging from nowhere as if they were coming out from under the rocks. All were in tune with their chores like an orchestra.

Jovita walked in a hurry and spoke to herself aloud. She was wearing a very clean and pressed hipil too, just like Amanda's mother, but with multi-colored flowery stitching instead and a full-body under-skirt. This was her everyday dress, but on Sundays and special occasions she wore an elaborate dress with large multi-colored flowers, double under-skirts equally embroidered, and beautiful gold-filigree jewelry. Jovita's hair was tied back with a ribbon, revealing a dark face highlighted by intelligent black eyes. Her face not beautiful, but open and gently lovely.

Jovita was in a bad mood. She did not like the new neighbor, "the Peon crow" she called her. She did not like throwing a party for her. She did not like hacienda owners in general. Jovita's husband, Cacho's father, had been in the rebel group that derailed a train between Tunkás and Temax, and later attacked nearby haciendas. At that time, the dictator Porfirio Diaz was in power in Mexico City, and there was turmoil across the Yucatan countryside. Cacho's father disappeared during those years leading up to the Revolution, and nobody in the government cared or did anything to help Jovita. She looked for him in jails and relatives' homes, but she knew he was dead, maybe lying in the middle of the Ceiva, the Yucatan jungle.

It was after her husband's disappearance that Jovita started as Amanda's nurse. She needed to stay all day at the Diaz home because of Norma's lack of interest in her new baby. Her easy personality and management abilities allowed her to take on running the whole household in just a few years.

Jovita was tireless. She was in charge of the house, the servants, the two Diaz girls, especially Amanda because of their life-long bond, and her own son Pedro and daughter Cacho. Norma Diaz spent most of her time holed up in her room.

Jovita liked working for the Diaz family. Aurelio Diaz was an importer who brought merchandise from Europe and sold luxury goods to the rich Merida families. Norma Cirerol Diaz, though, was from a rich hacienda owner's family, a class of people with whom it was hard for Jovita to work. Fortunately, Norma was never involved with the household decisions and her relatives never visited her.

In the Diaz household, everyone knew Jovita's political views, and she was quite open about trying to "educate" anyone willing to listen. She liked the new governor, Salvador Alvarado. He brought a new focus on poor workers and did not like the entrenched landowners. He nicknamed them la *Casta Divina*, the Divine Caste, making a joke of how this class considered themselves superior by birth and the lighter color of their skin.

Despite this, even the landowners grew to like the new governor. Thanks to him and the increase in the price of henequen, the Divine Caste of Yucatan earned millions in profits, so they put aside the irony of the nickname and began to use it among themselves.

The reason that people like Jovita liked Alvarado was that he had emancipated the peones and allowed Mayan Indians and other indigenous people to escape from 350 years of serfdom, officially ending a caste war that had been raging for over half a century. He set minimum wages for household workers and established a maximum workday of eight hours. "Yucatan is by far the most revolutionary Mexican state," Jovita proudly said to everyone. Just as proudly, she collected her salary and saved it for future years, one of the first generation of indigenous Mayans to be able to do this. Because of all this, Jovita had a picture of Alvarado in the kitchen and always kept fresh flowers in front of it as if he were a saint.

That day of the party, Jovita assigned without hesitation different tasks to the various workers. "Someone needs to clean the bird cages!" she shouted, referring to the twenty cages that surrounded the courtyard. "Set up the china, the silverware and the tables and chairs!" she shouted through the kitchen window to Ramona, one of the maids. Her voice created a melody among the whistles of twenty birds.

The cooks were preparing papat-zules, the "king's dish," a Mayan taco dish made from a pumpkin seed paste mixed with aromatic leaves and boiled eggs. The smell filled the house, accompanied by the clacking sound of the molcajete, a black stone utensil used to grind the seeds.

Amanda ran back to her bedroom without seeing Cacho again. They were both getting ready to go to school. In her room, Amanda discovered as always her clothes laid out on her bed. The hammock in which she slept was neatly knotted and hung on the wall, and a small bunch of xtabentum flowers was set on a nightstand to fill the room with the smell of honey. These small white flowers, each half size of Amanda's hand, had delicate petals formed in a bell or trumpet shape. The arrangement of them looked wild, because their stems were not straight but twisted in all directions. Deep green stems and leaves made up most of the arrangement, which made the pure color of the blossoms stand out all the more from the chaos.

Amanda's father Aurelio waited for her as always at the front door, wearing a light beige suit. He was not tall, but had a commanding presence dominated by light blue eyes the color of the Caribbean Sea. The fair skin of his face was always shaded by a redness in his cheeks and his full head of hair made him look young. He always walked Amanda to school on his way to his offices and warehouses.

The two of them were crossing the Mother's Park when a sudden noise of shattering glass attracted their attention. The noise came from the front of a small military prison, where a group of priests were demanding with loud shouts and foot pounding the return of the Blister Cross, an icon revered by many people because it had survived intact a devastating church fire.

"Give us back the Christ, you evil Salvador Alvarado! Give us back the Christ, sinner!" they shouted while banging on the prison doors.

Could this be the same Salvador Alvarado whom Jovita adored, who had fresh flowers set in front of his picture in the kitchen each day? The Liberator, the reason Yucatan was prospering and enjoying freedom for all? Amanda was baffled.

A large group gathered around the priests, and it was then that the prison doors opened and a military detail carrying a dozen different icons in their hands threw them without mercy into the middle of the cobblestone street. The various saints and virgins were shattered, never to be seen intact again. Once-beautiful artwork was scattered on the ground in hundreds of pieces.

The priests were forced by the soldiers to leave the streets, but a group of tearful women began picking up the destroyed pieces, carefully saving in their skirt hems the glass and clay remnants. Amanda noticed that one of these women was a good friend of Jovita's.

Amanda felt confused and asked her father for an explanation. He described to her the historic clash between the Catholic religion and the indigenous people's love for pagan icons, and how the government had implemented a separation of church and state.

"The Mayan people used to believe in many gods – the sun god, the rain god, the mother god, and so on. The Spanish came to this continent and introduced them to the true Catholic religion, with one god and many saints. Indians have mixed the two religions, venerating the saints as if they were gods."

Changing his tone he added, "Another thing to understand is that the government is afraid of the church." He finished his story without further explanation, as if he knew that he was wasting his time explaining to a child, grasped her hand, and continued the walk to Amanda's school.

What Amanda understood from all this was that the church had too much power, and that at some point in the past, the Indians had switched from multi-god culture to a multi-saint culture.

"It seems so unfair that they are destroying all these beautiful things. So the government was the cause of this suffering today?" she asked.

"Yes," said her father simply. Amanda could not understand how a man as loved as Alvarado could do such mean things. She knew only Jovita's passionate views and the distant intellectual opinions of her father, who described things as if they were happening on a far-off stage and as if the people involved were just wooden puppets. She wanted to understand more but was too young, and her eagerness was forgotten when they arrived at school.

Amanda would always remember that day for several reasons. First, for the successful prank. Later, for her first meeting with the new neighbor, who would change her life forever. And finally, because on that day she would begin to have political feelings too. That day would open her eyes to people's hunger for understanding and the different political views that would make someone a hero to some observers and a monster to others.

Chapter 3: Peregrina (The Pilgrim)

Merida, 1922

● ● ●

Peregrina, de ojos claros y divinos

(Lady Pilgrim, with divine light eyes)

y mejillas encendidas de arrebol,

(and bright rosy cheeks,)

mujercita de los labios purpurinos

(woman of small ruby lips)

y radiante cabellera como el sol

(and hair bright as the sun.)

Peregrina que dejaste tus lugares

(Lady pilgrim, who left your home)

los abetos y la nieve, y la nieve virginal

(of silver firs and snow, virgin snow)

y viniste a refugiarte en mis palmares

(and came here to find a refuge in my palm trees)

bajo el cielo de mi tierra, de mi tierra tropical.

(under the sky of my land, my tropical land.)

Las canoras, avecillas de mis prados,

(The canoras, little birds of my meadows,)

por cantarte dan sus trinos si te ven

(sing to you their trills if they see you)

y las flores de nectarios perfumados

(and the flowers with perfumed nectars)

te acarician y te besan en los labios y en la sien.

(caress and kiss you on the lips and temples.)

Cuando dejes mis palmares y mi tierra,

(When you leave my palms and my land,)

peregrina del semblante encantador,

(Lady pilgrim with the enchanted countenance,)

no te olvides, no te olvides de mi tierra..

(do not forget, do not forget my land...)

no te olvides, no te olvides de mi amor.

(do not forget, do not forget my love.)

- "Peregrina" by Luis Rosado Vega/Ricardo Palmerin

Yucatan folk song

Sometimes it is good to give up on impossible dreams, opening opportunities for new goals that, with the mature wisdom of age, can create new happiness and fulfillment.

On his way to meet his friend, Carlos Ancona saw that his beloved city, Merida, looked the same as before he left. The Revolution had not destroyed the stone streets or the white houses whose borders and beautiful windows came right up to the street. And, fortunately, the houses' open front doors still showed courtyards full of children, either shyly looking out at Carlos or playing on the ground with toy cars. Carlos smiled to see a group of barefoot kids in front of the market, grinning as they ate large pieces of a yellowish star-shaped fruit called canistel, which reflected the sunlight onto their faces.

The past few years had not been easy on Carlos, but he was happy to be back in his hometown and was sure that 1923 was going to be a good year for him. He needed to hurry to be on time for his meeting with Gualberto Carrillo Puerto, brother of the new governor of the state of Yucatan, Felipe Carrillo Puerto. Gualberto ran the transportation department, and had hinted at the possibility of a job for Carlos.

Carlos walked into the office just at the appointed time. Gualberto was sitting behind his desk with a large pile of papers in front of him.

"So, the famous liberator of the poor is back in town!" Gualberto shouted this as he stood up and extended his hand for a hard squeeze.

"Yes, I am here," Carlos said, his light blue eyes reflecting little anticipation.

"You look the same," Gualberto said, "but your long curly hair is gone, thank G--...Felipe."

"Ha," said Carlos." How is your Bolshevik brother?"

"He is working hard and winning the hearts of the people. He was the first governor to speak Mayan at his inauguration. You should have seen him. The people loved it. Now he is immersed in a project of land distribution to the indigenous people."

"I heard from my brother that we are not the first state to be doing this land distribution."

"But we are the one with the most farmed land. By the way, how is your brother Antonio?"

"He is good, still in Mexico City. But let's talk about the famous Felipe Carrillo Puerto. How is he dealing with the *Casta Divina*? Do they hate him?" asked Carlos.

"Well, they are appealing many of his actions to federal judges."

"He will be a good governor if he still has the same energy as when he and Antonio ran that newspaper together a few years ago."

"Well, yes, Felipe is still the same. But this time the government is different -- nobody is going to leave Merida in a hurry or go to jail. Felipe is a little more relaxed. Can you imagine that is possible for him?" Gualberto said this as he ran his hands through his full head of black curly hair. He was short and thin, with the narrow face of a fox and a firm mouth.

"He is a good politician," remarked Carlos. "For the record, I am more relaxed now too."

"I can't believe I am hearing this from you."

"I ran into a bit of a wall."

"And who was the builder? I hope it was not a woman."

"You know me better than that. No, I worked for Pancho Villa for a while."

By this time, Gualberto had invited Carlos to sit down on a little sofa that was next to his desk. This made it much easier for the short Gualberto to look at Carlos, as there was a large difference in height between the two men. Carlos was of medium height, with an unarranged posture but determined hands. His blue eyes stood out not because of their unusual color for Mexico, but because of their gentleness, which encouraged people to feel comfortable around him.

"How did that work out?" asked Gualberto.

"Well, we didn't spend much time discussing Anatole France or Voltaire."

"Be serious, please."

"I introduced myself to Villa and gave a little background on my father's writing skills and the job I did here working for Felipe and Antonio on the newspaper. He hired me to create his own personal newspaper."

"That sounds like just the type of thing that you would like to do."

"In the beginning, it was exciting. Villa spent some time educating me on his revolutionary ideas, the distribution of land, and the greatness of Pancho Villa. It was life in front of the campfire surrounded by beautiful women."

"Like peeling *habanero chiles* with your bare hands."

"What?" asked Carlos.

"Never mind. Just a sarcastic expression about your painful task. Go on."

"Anyway, things turned out badly. The first battle was thrilling, a great victory. Villa was like Attila in the fields. It's was my first encounter with the real Revolution and I was full of eagerness for equality and freedom. But the aftermath was something else entirely. Unarmed men were murdered and women raped without mercy. Meanwhile, I was instructed to take over the newspaper facilities and print articles about the greatness and sensitive charity of Pancho Villa. After a few such "victories," I deserted, if a journalist can desert the army."

"Well, nobody needs to know about that," Gualberto said. "But let's turn to business."

"You are going to help me with the Chichen-Itza-to-Uxmal highway project. We are going to need many tourist brochures about these beautiful cities. You can help with the writing and the logistics of publishing them, and will be in charge of dealing with important visitors, not only from around here but from all over the world."

"I am very interested. I certainly need a break from revolutionary thinking. And I know many stories of Uxmal and Chichen-Itza, folklore that I would love to put down into a book. Thanks, Gualberto."

"And thanks to my brother," said Gualberto, standing up.

"By the way," Gualberto added, "you should come with me this evening to a party in Progreso. Felipe is going to be there. There will be bonfires on the beach. The singer and composer Ricardo Palmerin is going to be there too, and he just might surprise Alma Reed with a new song."

"Alma Reed?"

"Of course, you have just arrived! Alma Reed is the new girlfriend of Felipe."

"Girlfriend?" asked Carlos with a surprised look on his face.

"Yes. Felipe is getting divorced. He is crazy for this woman."

"Who is she?"

"She is an American from California, in fact a writer like you. She had a newspaper column that gave legal advice to people with no resources, which included almost all the Mexican population of the area. She helped a 17-year-old Mexican kid who was on death row. She went to visit him at San Quentin, ran her story at the San Francisco Morning Call, got the governor to issue a stay of execution, and later helped to create a bill that prevented the hanging of minors."

"Impressive," Carlos said.

"There is more. She came to Merida as a special guest to research and write about the ruins at Chichen-Itza and Uxmal. She was interested in archeology and wanted to write an article about the Mayans. While she was here she met Edward Thompson, the American who had bought all the land around both areas."

"Oh yes, I remember my father telling me the story," said Carlos. I think he bought all the ruins for less than a hundred dollars, an area of many square miles."

"Well, she became good friends of this Thompson until she divulged his work in the cenote," said Gualberto, referring to a deep well that historically had been used by the Mayans as a site for sacrifices to Chac, the rain god. "Thompson had dredged it and was pulling up all sorts of jewelry and other artifacts that he was sending to a Boston museum."

"Did she write about this in the United States?"

"No, even better, she got him to put in writing what he was doing, which is now helping us bring all these national treasures back to Mexico."

"I can see why Felipe likes her. She fights for the underdog."

"Alma always has a funny story. When she first came to Merida, she arrived at the same time as the wife of an important executive. He had sent a Mariachi band to welcome his wife and serenade her. They played the one that says "---Alma mia sola siempre sola---. " Alma, not knowing much Spanish, thought that they were singing especially for her, instead of a song about the soul. She made a big show of thanking the band, which really confused the poor wife, who thought that the music was for her."

"Funny," chuckled Carlos. "I can imagine the wife's face."

"Felipe and Alma like to tell the story when people first meet Alma. Now Felipe has asked Palmerin to write a song especially for her, and there is a talk that he may propose."

"Politics and romance, combined with music. Only in Yucatan. Anyway, I would love to go to the party, of course."

"Great. I will also introduce you to my good friend Julieta Diaz Cirerol. She will be there with her sister Amanda, a smart pretty teenager whom I know you will like."

"Are they related to the Cirerol family that..."

"Yes," interrupted Gualberto. "But I don't think that the daughters know anything about that."

"I like Mr. Diaz," said Carlos. "I met him a couple of times at his store."

"He will be there too. The young ladies need to be accompanied by a respectable adult."

"Wouldn't that normally be the mother?" asked Carlos.

"Yes but the mother keeps mostly to herself. The father is more sociable, and once he gets a good conversation going will hardly pay attention to where his daughters are."

"Well, I can't wait. But I should be going." Finally, Carlos stood up, and the two men said their goodbyes and parted with a friendly hug.

Carlos felt good on the way back to his house. He would be able to relax and stop worrying about depending on his father and brother. His politics had led him to complicated and interesting life experiences, but he was getting uncomfortable as an adult depending on money from his family.

Carlos decided to enjoy his Merida and walk home. The day was scorching. He was crossing a long block when, without noticing, he walked across the entrance to a home construction site and ended up in the way of a worker who was carrying a large stone on his back, forcing the worker to set down the stone. The foreman was standing close by and berated the worker for putting down the stone. The worker, a Mayan, took his hat off and apologized, moving his hand around the hat and staring at the ground in resignation.

Carlos' heart sank. These were the people he had wanted to help all his life, and by accepting this writing job, it would mean turning his back on that cause to work as a bureaucrat.

Carlos had lived for his ideas. He had traveled Mexico during the Revolution, and wanted to record the amazing lives of its heroes. He had traveled with a number of different military groups and suffered the joys and the pains of war. He had been shocked at the changes in the personalities of the "people's generals" when they got power, but the war needed strong men.

Now Carlos was standing in the middle of a fight between the classes not knowing where to go. He saw the good and bad of each of the sides. He wasn't getting any younger, and his grand ideas were giving him only problems and an empty wallet. He knew it was hard to fight against the rich conservatives, especially since some of them had been his friends and schoolmates growing up. But they cared about nothing but themselves. They were set for life, and their sole focus was on preserving the system that had made them rich.

Carlos knew that fresh ideas were in power and he was sure that things were going in the right direction for this poor Mexico that had seen so much suffering. Mexico had so much fertile and virgin land that in few years it would bring prosperity for all. Mexico did not need him for this, but at the same time would always need him. He could stay in this constant loop or, for the first time in his life, step out, breathe, get out of the dizziness, and enjoy life.

Chapter 4: The Magician's Pyramid (Uxmal)

Merida, 1922

An old sorcerer hatched a boy from a large black egg, and by his first birthday the boy had grown to an adult dwarf.

One day, the dwarf found a percussion instrument and played it so loudly that it was heard throughout the entire kingdom, even by the king of Uxmal. The king took this as an omen that he would lose power over his kingdom and challenged the dwarf to a number of tasks, including the building of a pyramid in a single night. The dwarf succeeded in all of them with the help of the old sorcerer.

His last task was to break a very hard coconut shell over the top of his head. He broke a whole basketful of them. The king tried to match his rival's task but died after hitting the first shell.

Thus began the reign of the magician dwarf. His pyramid can be found in Uxmal.

- Mayan Legend, as told by Carlos Ancona

Why put off the enjoyment of love?

Amanda and Julieta sat on the patio of their home, drinking horchata, a fresh drink made from white rice. As sisters, they looked much alike, but Julieta was taller and more fair, and she radiated self-confidence. Both sisters had hazel eyes that changed color when the sun hit them and the same smile that brought all their features together in harmony.

It was about the time of day when Gualberto and Carlos usually showed up. Amanda had met Carlos several months ago at a party that Felipe Carrillo Puerto had thrown for Alma Reed. The party had been full of smart conversation, utopian ideas, and a lot of talk about possible socialist projects for Yucatan.

Carlos was a great conversationalist who held everyone's attention with his fascinating stories. He had seemed to like Amanda, but she had not been sure. Since then, Carlos had come to her house almost daily and was polite to everyone in the household. But he had never approached Amanda with anything more than friendship, and there was a ten-year age gap between them. Still, she felt special when important people like Carlos visited her house, and she enjoyed having deep conversations.

The world was changing fast and there were many new ideas to discuss. The advantage to Amanda of having her father, rather than her mother, as her main companion was the freedom to talk to men. Her father's circle included mature, worldly men, a sharp contrast to the insipid teenagers Amanda otherwise would see. Her father was especially happy with the visits of Carlos Ancona and hoped that soon there would be a proposal.

This time Gualberto arrived first, coming through the big doors to the central patio with a grin, holding Alma Reed's hand.

"Look who I found on my way here, our beautiful pilgrim, the Governor's future wife," said Gualberto, taking off his hat and dabbing his forehead with a white handkerchief.

Alma stood next to him wearing a fashionable white dress, her heart-shaped face shaded by a broad-brimmed hat. Gualberto's comment embarrassed Alma; her face got a little red and she nervously pulled her hair to one shoulder, making it shine like chestnut silk.

"So, what new story do you have for us, Gualberto?" asked Amanda after greeting both of them and motioning them to two chairs.

"Oh, an old one, but Alma hasn't heard it yet."

"Well?" said Julieta as she offered glasses of horchata to the guests.

"Do you remember a few years ago, how they were hanging people in Merida's central plaza?"

"I thought we were going to hear a funny story!" interrupted Julieta.

"It is funny, perhaps in the sense that Edgar Allan Poe can be, but let me finish. Anyway, it was a common sight, and the bodies were always pinned with little notes that explained the reasons for the hangings – a murderer, a horse thief, etc. Then one morning when I was on my way to work, I saw a funny sight. During the night, someone had hung chickens in the same place."

"Chickens with their crimes named?" Alma asked.

"Yes. One chicken's note said 'corn thief' and another one's said 'egg breaker.'"

"Oh, that's different. But I don't think it's funny," said Julieta. "It sounds like they were mocking death, trying to make a joke in poor taste. It seems offensive, in a way."

"I don't think anyone was trying to be offensive," Amanda said. "This just shows you how our people are. We mock death all the time, especially on All Saints Day in November, when we constantly make jokes about how people are going to die. Remember when a friend wrote that poem about me dying in a bizarre way? The verse had a perfect rhyme!"

"Who could forget, a beautiful poem about you being hit by a runaway drunken donkey?" smiled Julieta.

"Let's change the topic or I will be forced to remember the poem that someone once wrote for you," Amanda said, teasing Julieta.

"So, Alma, I hear that you are going back to the United States to prepare for the wedding," Julieta said, quickly going along with Amanda's request.

"Yes," said Alma. "The wedding will be here but I am going to New Orleans so I can more easily invite my relatives and friends, as well as pick up my dress."

"While you are doing that, the rest of us have another party in Progreso. We are leaving today," Amanda said. "My father cannot go. We are going to stay at the house of my good friend Olivia, and her mother will take us to the party."

The conversation was interrupted at this moment by a loud noise coming from the back of the house, from the area of the servants' quarters. Just then, Carlos Ancona showed up through the service corridor, with a fresh tortilla in his hand.

"What happened?" everyone said.

"I don't know," said Carlos. "Maybe Jovita finally knocked down that crow's nest that they found on top of the laundry room. I saw that they were using a tall ladder for something." Carlos took a bite of his tortilla.

"What were you doing there?" asked Amanda.

"I was hungry and wanted one of the fresh tortillas that Jovita always has ready. I snuck in there before saying hello," said Carlos, still holding half of the tortilla.

"Are you crazy? We can feed you more than just a tortilla. Please ask for anything and I will have it made it for you," Amanda said. "This morning I saw some maids with red hands, so my guess is that we are having cochinita or some kind of pibil recipe for dinner. I can get you some." Amanda's face was slightly flushed.

"Don't worry -- I just wanted a snack and there is nothing better than a fresh warm tortilla with salt. It's more appetizing than you think," Carlos said, finishing the last piece with a satisfied smile.

"Now that we are all here," said Alma, "I want to talk to you about Lupe. This morning I woke up after a strange dream. I told Lupe about this dream at breakfast."

"Lupe, the girl who helps you at home?" interrupted Julieta.

"Yes. She hasn't stop crying since I told the story, and she wants to take me to what sounds like a witch, or to a priest if I am more open to that," said Alma.

"So, what did you dream?" asked Carlos.

"I dreamed that I was at a street party dancing with Felipe and we were just having a good time. As we swung around the dance floor we accidentally bumped into a table covered with jars and vases, and they all broke."

"OHHH," said everybody at once.

"What? Is there something I don't understand? It was actually beautiful -- the pieces became butterflies that flew over to a wall and arranged themselves into a beautiful landscape."

"Well," said Carlos, "it is not the butterflies that are important, but the breaking of the jars. People from around here think that if you dream that a jar gets broken, death is following you, and a loved one will soon die."

"In that case, I am happy to say that I don't believe in such things," said Alma with a smile on her face. "I do want to calm Lupe, though."

"The only way that she will forget about the dream is if you do the things that she told you," said Julieta with a long face. "And you need to take this a little more seriously."

"I will go with you to see the witch," volunteered Amanda. "It will be interesting, and I have always wondered what exactly the witches do."

"Don't wait," someone boomed, causing everyone to turn. Jovita stood in the middle of the patio with another jar of horchata and a finger pointed at Alma. "You must go as soon as possible."

"I will try to do something, Jovita. Don't worry," said Alma.

"Jovita, now that you are here can you please get our bags ready? We are going to my friend Olivia's hacienda," Julieta said in a haughty tone.

"Yes," said Amanda. "And please tell Cacho that she needs to be ready soon."

"I will get the bags ready, but Cacho will not be able to go. A few hours ago the Peon crow..."

"She means the Peon widow, our neighbor," interrupted Amanda, making a face at Jovita.

"She came crying like a baby to your father, complaining about the lack of quality service and the need for someone to read to her, because her vision is failing and she sometimes sits for days without any entertainment. Your father thought it would be a good idea to send Cacho to help her and read to her for a couple of hours a day, because she is the best reader around here. So that will make it impossible for her to travel with you for a while or until your father finds someone else who can help the widow," ended Jovita.

"What I am going to do without Cacho?" Amanda said with genuine sadness.

"Hey, I have an idea," said Alma with a smile. "Let's take a picture of her for you to take with you. I should have time to develop it before you go to the hacienda."

"That sounds great," Amanda said. "We should call Cacho and take the picture." There was a bit of commotion while chairs were re-arranged, and Jovita went to call Cacho.

Cacho showed up a short time later, looking radiant in a gray dress and with an especially intense look in her eyes. Her brother Pedro came with her to help move the chairs. He was wearing an open shirt with his sleeves rolled up. Pedro apologized for his attire, but explained the work he was doing at the back of the house. He was, in fact, removing the crow's nest, which turned out to be full of jewelry and watches that had disappeared in the house over the past several years.

Pedro had a smile so wide that it covered half his face, and his timid gaze made his masculinity stand out even more. Sunlight gleamed from his body with hues of chocolate, honey and roasted almonds. The women in the room all felt little knots in their stomachs and their eyes followed every move he made, looking like a black jaguar stalking the jungle.

In due course, Amanda and Cacho decided to stand next to their favorite tree while Alma set up the camera for the right light and angle. They were all ready to take the picture and Alma had asked everyone to smile when Jovita interrupted. She reminded Cacho about the hipil for Amanda. Cacho had worked on it for weeks and it was ready for Amanda to review before the finishing touches were put on before the upcoming holiday season. Cacho ran toward the house and out of the frame just as Alma took the picture.

The moment was gone, and this group would never be together again. The butterflies in Alma's dream would fly in all directions. Some would lose their way, and the others would find their way together, like generations of monarch butterflies returning to the birthplace of their ancestors.

***

The door opened and a black figure entered the room and carefully closed the door. As eyes adjusted to the lack of light, a hand guided the figure to the floor. The two figures were so desperate for each other that they were soon free of their clothing. Their caresses covered every inch of skin – the firmness of round breasts and the soft curved ends of arched backs. Their bodies fit together as precisely as a puzzle.

Fire and water, clouds and rock, these two bodies were as different as can be. Their sweat mixed, creating a new stronger scent, tasty to their hungry lips. The attraction that they had to each other created fireworks, and steam boiled from their bodies.

They paused several times to stare into each other's eyes. Their desire strong, they finished quickly. But they stayed together, each silently stealing the breath from the other.

Flour and chocolate, cinnamon and sugar, the dessert of life.

Chapter 5: Xtabey

Merida, 1922

The envious Utz-Colel called the dark spirits and asked to return to the Earth. She became the dreaded Xtabey, who tricked people and took them to their deaths.

- *Continuation of the Xtabentum story – Mayan Legend*

When a time bomb of collected sorrow and resentment explodes, its devastation can reach more than those immediately involved. Its victims carry away a contamination in their bodies, ready to infect those with whom they come in contact.

Amanda was coming home after three weeks at Olivia's hacienda. Julieta was not yet ready to return, but Amanda could not wait to get back home and talk to Cacho, and the last weeks at the hacienda had dragged on. She had made good progress on the tablecloth she was crocheting, but was ready to get back to the social life surrounding the upcoming Christmas and New Year's holidays. She missed the daily visits of Carlos, too. He had not tried to contact her in all the time that she had been away or even send her a message through friends who had visited Olivia during the weeks.

Amanda's heart was lonely and she felt weary. She liked Carlos' attention. She was comfortable with him, and thinking about him felt like a familiar song humming through her head.

She guessed that the reason for Carlos' silence was the difficult political situation. General Adolfo de la Huerta was attempting to overthrow the Mexican government. The position of Felipe Carrillo Puerto in the government of Yucatan was precarious.

Felipe Carrillo Puerto was well accepted and loved throughout the state, and no one at Olivia's hacienda had worried about the government. They were sure that bad news from Mexico City would not affect the Yucatan governor.

Felipe Carrillo Puerto was a good politician, but Amanda worried that the information she had received was not accurate, as it came from a group of teenage girls who thought that politics was not a proper subject for girls. She felt mature for her age and did not consider herself a normal teenager.

Back in Merida, the house was a little too silent for this time of the day. Amanda even felt that the birds were not singing as usual, and when she entered the courtyard, she noticed that the doors were all closed, as if the house did not want to hear any more news from the outside. She walked to her mother's room and saw that it was completely dark, with the curtains blocking every ray of light. She debated opening her mother's door, but her instincts made her back out and walk to the servants' quarters.

Finding the kitchen empty, Amanda became alarmed. Jovita would never let everyone off, unless something terrible had happened. Panic ran through her body like a deep pain, as if she had discovered herself stepping on glass. She started yelling for her father, like a lost toddler.

"Papi, Papi! Where are you?" Then to Jovita, "Nana, Nana! Is anyone home?"

A door finally opened and Ramona, one of the housekeepers, came out of Cacho's room with her hand over her mouth, and ran to embrace Amanda. She was crying hard and shouting, "Xtabey did it, Xtabey did it!" She pulled Amanda into Cacho's room. Amanda could see that someone was lying in an awkward position on the hammock in a corner of the room. It was Cacho.

"Jovita gave her something to put her to sleep," Ramona said, sobbing every other word. "And we tried to make her comfortable in a position where she will not get hurt anymore."

Cacho was face-down with her arms and legs hanging down from the hammock. She looked like an animal being carried back from the hunt.

Amanda was shaking as she walked to stand next to Cacho, and saw that her back was covered with open wounds as thick as fingers. Her skin was flayed across all of her back, leaving only the redness of rare meet. Someone had applied a greenish powder, which made it look as though the sores were infected.

Amanda's heart sank as she took hold of Cacho's hand. She rubbed Cacho's cheek, which also had some small marks on it. Cacho's face was wet with the combination of melting tears and sickly sweat. Amanda felt the room spin and almost fainted, but she reminded herself that she needed to be strong for the moment and recovered her composure a few seconds later.

"She can't stay here. We need to take her to the hospital."

"Nobody is here," said Ramona. "Jovita already brought a doctor, who recommended only keeping the cuts uncovered and clean. Jovita then visited one of her friends and brought back the ingredient that we had been applying to her back every hour," said Ramona.

"But where is Jovita?" Amanda could not believe that Jovita had left Cacho in this state. "And who did this to Cacho?" Amanda asked, remembering Ramona's first words when she saw her. Ramona said that it was Xtabey, but with the stress of the moment, she could not think why.

"Oh, Miss Amanda. There is more, a lot more," said Ramona, looking down.

"Okay, you are going to tell me everything, but first we need to move her to my bed. I am worried that her hands and feet will swell if she stays in that position any longer. I will try to wake her up and make her walk to my room," said Amanda in a serious voice.

Amanda went back to Cacho's hammock and started whispering sweet words in her ear. She saw that Cacho's eyes started to move in a small response. At last, Cacho woke up and looked directly into Amanda eyes. She smiled like a little girl.

"I finished your dress Amanda. Oh, it is so pretty; you are really going to like it. It has all your favorite colors and..."

"Cacho," Amanda interrupted, "I need your help. You are going to stand up and walk with me to my room."

"No problem," said Cacho, and she suddenly stood up as if nothing had happened. She was in another world but the smile melted from her face, and a terrible scream came from her mouth. She fell to the floor, landing on her hands and knees like a crawling baby, shouting, "No, no, please, stop! I'm sorry, I'm sorry!"

"Jovita gave her some kind of drink for the pain and she has been saying strange things all day," Ramona said.

Amanda kneeled down and helped Cacho stand up, almost carrying her, surprised at the extra strength that she had. Amanda looked at her. She was awake, and her eyes looked rational, not mad as before.

"Where were you? Why couldn't you help me?" Cacho whispered while a stream of tears poured down her face.

Amanda and Ramona walked Cacho to Amanda's room and laid her on the bed. In a moment, she seemed to be asleep. But then, she opened her eyes, touched the pillow and said to Amanda, "We were supposed to be sisters, but it was just all a lie. I will never be like you."

Amanda rushed out of the room as fast as she could. She thought again that she might faint, and did not want to do it in front of Cacho. She sat on the floor. Sounds seemed to disorient her and she felt she could not breathe. She could not think at all. Her mind had not yet registered Cacho's words, but later those words would strike and scar her heart, and she would find that she had no way of mending it.

Amanda came back to reality when Ramona came out of the room.

"What happened? Who attacked us? Is my father all right? Where is everyone?" said Amanda in a high voice, trying to control the trembling in her words.

"Oh Miss Amanda, your father is fine, but it has been a nightmare here these last two days..."

"Two days? This had been going on for two days and I didn't know?" groaned Amanda.

"Well, you were gone and your father needed to go to the police to report Cacho's situation and try to save Pedro," said Ramona, casting her eyes down in an apology.

"Pedro? What happened to him?"

"He is in jail..."

"What? Why?"

"Miss Amanda, let me explain from the beginning. Please, it will be easier."

"Yes, of course, Ramona. But don't take too long like you always do, and try to give me the simple version."

"I will, Miss Amanda. Do you remember when you left, that Cacho was going to work with our neighbor for a couple of days?" asked Ramona, finally settling down into a normal voice.

"The widow Peon, of course I remember. She was the reason that Cacho didn't come with me to the hacienda. She needed some kind of help reading," said Amanda a little too fast, showing just how nervous she was.

"Yes. Cacho went there to help, not just with reading but with a holiday party the widow had one evening. Everything went well until the next day. She had used her good silverware and there was a spoon missing," said Ramona with tears in her eyes.

Amanda knew the end of the story immediately. She knew that type of person and the methods they used to keep their servants in line.

"The Peon widow whipped Cacho, trying to find out about her tea spoon," Amanda said in a rage. She could see the image clearly.

"We heard Cacho's screams all the way here. Jovita and your father ran to help her, but it was already too late. Cacho was unconscious in the floor when they arrived and the widow was on top of her whipping her small body without mercy. Your father was outraged. He told her that he was going to denounce her and that he would make sure she paid by spending the rest of her days in a dungeon. The widow laughed. She knew it was all just words. She knew she would never go to jail for beating a servant."

"We brought Cacho back here and took care of her, but it was late and your father decided to wait until the next day to go to the police station. He calmed Jovita, assuring her that there would be justice. He knew that the widow would not flee. She did not have anywhere to go and had no one to help her. But most of all, she thought that she had done nothing wrong. She was probably sleeping calmly in her bed."

"Your father never did go to the police, though," she continued. "The next morning the police were all over the Peon widow's house. Your father thought it was a trick of the widow's to try to win the police over with a false story, but when he went to her house to try to straighten out the story, he found that someone had killed the widow during the night. She had died from a gunshot right in the middle of her forehead. Whoever killed her wanted to destroy her evil mind."

Amanda was too stunned to speak.

"She died in the same room where she had whipped Cacho. Her blood is now mixed with Cacho's blood for eternity. Later when the cleaning people went to the room, they found out that Cacho's blood was easily cleaned but that the widow's blood had stained the floor with an ugly mark that will be impossible to erase and will repulse people for years to come. Xtabey was jealous of Cacho, but for once received her own punishment back," ended Ramona with tears in her eyes.

"Ramona, that doesn't make sense. Xtabey is supposed to be an unseen beautiful witch and the widow Peon was an old lady," Amanda said with a little anger in her voice.

"Yes, but then how do you explain how she had the strength to do all that damage to Cacho?" replied Ramona.

"Hate," said Amanda. "Hate and the sweet modesty of Cacho." Tears covered Amanda's face, and she did nothing to try to stop them. She imagined Cacho just standing there in disbelief as the widow began to hit her. Cacho would try to show her strength and not let anyone, especially the Peon widow, break her spirit.

"They are accusing Pedro of the killing!" Ramona broke in.

Time stopped for Amanda, her vision blurred and her heart raced. She could not take it anymore. She walked out to the garden and threw up, her entire body shaking.

Of course they would blame Pedro, and maybe he was guilty -- Amanda herself would have been thrown into a rage if she had been present. On the other hand, Pedro was the gentlest person in the world. It looked like that ugly old witch had destroyed two lives in a moment without giving it a second thought. And now she had died alone, abandoned by everyone and with rancor in her heart.

Amanda made herself calm down. Cacho needed her. Making a great effort, she went back to her room to check on

Cacho. She was resting quietly, and Amanda fell asleep in the chair next to her own bed, where Cacho slept.

Amada waited all the next day for her father. She wanted to go find him, but knew it was a bad idea to leave Cacho alone. Jovita was with him and they were doing all that could be done to save Pedro.

As she thought about it, Amanda was sure that Pedro, the Pedro she had known all her life, could not do something like that. Not only was he was a gentle person, but also she was almost sure he had never held a gun in his hand. He wanted to be a doctor, someone who saved people. She sighed as she thought about his direct gaze with those beautiful black cat eyes.

She fell asleep again in the chair next to Cacho, not noticing the coming and going of Ramona. The morning sun woke her up, and with it came the visit of her father. She hugged him fiercely. "Thanks for staying on the good side, Papi."

"I am always on the side of reason, Amanda, but you need to sit down. There is a great deal that I want to tell you," he said in a solemn tone.

They sat down on the only two chairs available in her room, the ones that she and Cacho used to share for hours while they discussed their goals and dreams or their everyday homework. Cacho still slept on the bed, but her face now looked more relaxed, as if she were in a normal dream, not one forced by medication. Her back looked a little better, too.

"Amanda," her father said, "yesterday afternoon they arrested Felipe Carrillo Puerto."

Amanda was shocked; she was waiting for more information about Pedro and never expected more bad news. This was too much.

"How? When?" asked Amanda, holding her breath.

"Someone betrayed him. In the end, many people abandoned him. He was captured along with three of his brothers and eight of his friends at the coast of El Cuyo as he was trying to escape toward Cuba, or maybe Quintana Roo."

Amanda thought of the irony of life. Felipe Carrillo Puerto was captured at one of the prettiest places in Yucatan, a flamingo paradise. El Cuyo was the place where the birds escaped to nest, the place to start a new life.

"This has been going on for a couple of weeks," her father began.

"Oh Papi," Amanda said coming back from her thoughts. "I can't believe that you left me at Olivia's hacienda. I did not know anything."

"Calm down," said her father, holding her shoulder. "Your friend Olivia's hacienda is one of the safest places to be right now. Her family is not really into politics and their land is too small to make a difference with the other hacienda owners. Mr. Lara is well loved by his workers, too. They would never do anything to harm the family. This may be the start of another revolution, and I wanted you to be safe."

He continued: "You can see the predicament I have been in, trying to save Pedro and get him out of jail at a time when nobody cares about his situation."

"I care," Amanda said. "We need to do something different like..."

"Wait a second, there is more. Pedro is now free."

"Really? That's great!"

"But Carlos is in jail instead of him," interrupted her father.

"What? Was he with Felipe Carrillo Puerto at El Cuyo?"

"No," said her father. "This is very strange.... He went to the police department and turned himself in as the killer of the widow Peon."

Tears came to Amanda eyes. "Only a noble person like Carlos would do something like that to save Pedro. I guess he thought that it would be easier for him to get out of jail than Pedro." Amanda thought that she would never be able to make such a selfless sacrifice.

"We don't know, Amanda. I have not talked to him at all in the past weeks. Carlos told many of his friends that he knew that Felipe was in jail, and some of his friends think that he wanted to be in jail at the same time as Felipe Carrillo Puerto to help him escape. He is being held at the new secure jail that Carrillo Puerto himself had rebuilt."

"He is so good," Amanda said, thinking about Carlos and having a warm feeling inside her for the first time in days.

"I don't know, Baby. When I finally talked to Pedro, he swore to me that he had not killed the widow. In fact, that night I had sent him to deliver one of my products to a house in Progreso. He told me that he arrived there late that night, spent the night in Progreso, and arrived back in the morning only to be arrested just as he walked into our house. He didn't know at first why he was in jail, that the widow was dead, or even that Cacho had been hurt."

"This means that the real killer is free, Papi. Maybe it was one of the other workers. Many of them hated that woman and love Cacho." Amanda felt color coming back to her face for the first time since this all began. "Where is Pedro?" she asked.

"I sent him to the United States," said her father, looking into her eyes to see her reaction.

Amanda was silent for a moment, thinking, then said in a very slow and controlled voice, "I guess it was the best for him. We can't take any chance of him going back to jail, and the casta divina would hound him forever."

Now their conversation came to an end. Cacho had awakened and stood in the middle of the room looking at them while her red puffy eyes shed a river of tears, dampening her loose outfit.

It was clear that Cacho had heard a great deal, and Amanda and her father tried to console her. Cacho stood there crying, and no matter how they tried to make her sit back on the bed, she refused, only moving her head from side to side without a single word. Amanda thought that even with all her injuries she looked very beautiful and fragile. She wanted to protect Cacho, but so far had proven very bad at it.

Amanda's father finally got Cacho to sit and calm down a bit. She went back to sleep after an hour of sobbing, and Amanda heard the rest of the story from her father.

Back in her chair next to Cacho, Amanda thought about the additional details she had learned from her father. Felipe, his brothers and his friends had argued about whether to flee the country or just hide in the jungle. They could run to Quintana Roo, where the governor was friendly. Then they were informed that there was a ship out near El Cuyo that was willing to take them to Havana, and it seemed too good to pass up.

Felipe had left Merida in a rush, thinking that it was just temporary. He had little time to prepare or to lay his hands on money. He sold or traded personal possessions, including his gold watch, for the transportation. He remembered Alma Reed, though; among his possessions when he was captured was her photo. They were supposed to get married in just a few weeks.

Felipe had seemed close to escape. But after enduring several scorching days with mosquitoes eating them alive and finally reaching the beach, they faced the malfunction of the boats that were supposed to take them out to sea and the ship that would take them to Havana. Later, they learned that the enemy had uncovered their plans and sabotaged the boats.

He and his supporters could have resorted to guns, but Felipe did not want to use violence against his own people. "They were just following orders," he reportedly said of his captors.

The coup was not enjoying much success and was said to be running short of money for its military operations. But that would not help Felipe Carrillo Puerto. He and his party faced prison and possible martyrdom.

Amanda thought about all this bad news, all coming fast, and was sure that more things would come soon. When a stream of bad luck hits, it is hard to break the chain, or as Jovita would say, "It always rains when it is wet." She looked at the black sky and hoped for better weather.

Chapter 6: The Way to Xibalba

Merida, 1923

The way to Xibalba, the Mayan underworld, is long and challenging. One must navigate rivers of blood, great currents, and sharp spines.

- ***From the Popol Vuh, the book of Mayan mythology***

The cell was dark and the humidity heavy, especially at night. The walls felt wet to the touch, and the changes in temperature were drastic from day to night.

Carlos' own Xibalba was consuming him with emptiness and stillness. Getting in was easy, but the way out looked impossible. Ironically, this was a beautiful, almost castle-like building with turrets and battlements, sentry boxes and lookouts.

Carlos' cell was small and simple, gray and plain. The jail had many cells, and he was in the least secure section. Political prisoners were on the secure side, with many soldiers protecting the place; killers were not that dangerous.

He spent most of each day looking out his window at the interior courtyard of the prison. He was trying to identify or guess the place where they were holding Felipe Carrillo Puerto. There was a great deal of activity in the courtyard, many new soldiers moving in and out, and those standing in the courtyard cleaning their weapons in the sun.

His captors interrogated Carlos every afternoon. Around four o'clock one afternoon his jailors walked him through the halls to the main military quarters, going from one side of the jail to the other, which helped him to see more of the jail and its security. They left him in a room where a small officer with a large dark mustache awaited him. The officer asked Carlos to repeat his name and confirm that he was the killer of Rosaura Peon Hurtado, but before Carlos could answer, loud steps, which echoed and bounced off the stone walls in a dramatic sound, interrupted the interview. It was the sound of a firing squad taking prisoners to the main courtyard for execution.

The officer opened the window to watch the show, as if ignoring Carlos' presence. He was smirking.

There were eleven prisoners in the courtyard, lined up to face the firing squad. Carlos jumped out of his chair, recognizing Felipe and Gualberto among the men. Two soldiers who had been standing near the door sprang forward, grabbed him, and tied him back to his chair. The mustached officer made sure Carlos was positioned so he could see everything.

All that was left for Carlos to do was to scream a loud "No!" People from the courtyard could hear him and he thought he recognized Felipe's voice shouting "Viva Yucatan! Please take care of my Indians!" just before the word "fire" was ordered.

But there was silence -- nothing happened. No gunshots, no bodies collapsing to the ground, no smoke racing up into the air.

The officers began to laugh, hard. Carlos could see the white faces of his friends, who were standing straight and without pleading, heads held high, proud.

"I guess you like this Felipe Carrillo Puerto guy," the officer said. "Don't worry, we are not barbarians. He is going to have a trial and..."

Carlos stopped listening. He had mixed feelings. On the one hand, he was in a state of shock from the scene he had just witnessed. On the other, he was happy to find out that Felipe and all his friends were alive. He needed to find a way to communicate with Felipe Carrillo Puerto. Carlos noticed that they took the group of prisoners to the end of the left side of the building, so now he knew which windows to watch. He recalled noticing a pair of eyes staring from one of those windows earlier in the morning; if they reappeared, he would try to communicate.

However, the eyes did not reappear, and the jail became silent. From outside the walls he could hear the December celebrations, and the particular noise of the gasoline trams used around the city as public transportation.

Days came slowly and the pattern never changed, as he looked out his window day after day. Carlos started to look forward to his meals, which were always beans and rice, plus occasionally a few pieces of pork. His mouth watered just thinking of the delicious Yucatan dishes made with pork, rice, black beans, lime, radish and cilantro. Nearby, people were eating dishes like this at their homes for supper. He felt ashamed to be thinking about his stomach and tried to concentrate on his escape instead.

No one had visited Carlos yet, but he assumed that this was because his jailors would not allow it. Carlos hoped that someone had informed his brother, and that he would find his way in. He would help with lawyers and political influence.

The old man who brought Carlos his food started to make eye contact with him, but never spoke. He was the typical Mayan Indian: small, with a disproportionately large head, and very fine black hair. The first time that he brought the food, he barely looked at Carlos, but day-by-day he became more familiar, and after some days, he was smiling back.

"You have a nice smile," Carlos adventured to say one day while the man was dropping the dish onto a small table that Carlos had in his room. He smiled back. "Where are you from? What is your name?" However, the old man just rushed out of the room without an answer, leaving Carlos alone once again.

Later that night, Carlos heard a small knock on his door. "Juan, from Motul," said a thick voice through the door. "Don't speak too loudly. Right now nobody is around because it is late, but a soldier does come around once in a while."

"Thanks," said Carlos. "My name is Carlos Ancona."

"I know who you are. Are you a friend of Felipe Carrillo Puerto?"

"Yes. How did you know?" Carlos asked, a bit surprised.

"I was outside the room when they played that sick joke on Felipe Carrillo Puerto and his comrades, and I saw your face. It was the face of a friend in pain." He paused for a moment, then continued: "I have been trying to switch my work to the other side of the prison, but almost everyone there is from De La Huerta's army. I have been working at the prison for almost two years now as the cook's helper. But they are running out of people so I am doing this job too, but only with the less important prisoners."

"I guess it has been extra hard for you, being from Motul and having Felipe Carrillo Puerto in jail," Carlos said, hearing the strange echo of his voice in the cell and lowering it further so that no one else would hear him.

"Yes. It's funny because in a way I have been following him. We are both from Motul. I was working at the Dzununcan hacienda when he destroyed the wall that prevented the Mayan villagers from passing through, the first time that he was put in jail. And I was in Merida's main plaza when he gave his first Mayan speech after he became governor. I got this job and never thought that he would end up here." By now, Carlos was used to the low voice and had positioned himself exactly opposite the point from which Juan's voice came.

"You seem like a peaceful man. Why are you working in a jail? Carlos asked.

"I am here because of deception and ignorance. When I lived in Motul, I worked at the Franciscan monastery, helping in the kitchen. This was during that time when a statue of Jesus Christ began crying in the middle of the day. I actually saw how water came from his face. The priests called it a miracle. They told us that it was a sign to make us work harder on some repairs underway at the church, and that Jesus was sad because his people continued some rituals to the old gods. This was back before Felipe Carrillo Puerto became governor," Juan said, stopping to take a long breath. Carlos thought that he had heard the same story from Amanda, but did not want to interrupt Juan. This relationship could be very helpful to him.

"One day, people from the government came to the church to investigate the miracle. Without warning, a soldier cut the statue in half with a sword and all could see a water-soaked cloth that with the change of temperatures sweated through the wood and covered the outside part of the figure with water.

"I felt betrayed. My own sister had given a week of her husband's salary to the church to celebrate the miraculous Christ. It was then that I decided to abandon the church and work for the government, and made my way to Merida. I worked a few different jobs until a couple of years ago I learned that they were looking for a cook's helper here, and I took the job." Juan ended his story with a sad voice as if he regretted every event in it.

"That is an incredible story, but you know, maybe you are here for a reason. You need to help me; you could be the one who saves Felipe Carrillo Puerto and gets him out of jail," Carlos said, unintentionally raising his voice a little.

Carlos held his breath waiting for a response, and after a few moments, Juan said, "I will try, but it will be difficult."

"He was so close to escape, too," Carlos adventured, after a long silent gap, hoping that Juan was still there.

"I heard that he was already on a boat, but the motor didn't work," Juan said.

"I heard that he actually jumped out of the boat and swam, just to give himself up to his pursuers. I cannot believe that his people betrayed him; some of his militia took easy money instead of a chance for a prosperous life for their people. He did so much for them, schools, free medical services and best of all, he taxed the Catholic Church." Carlos stopped, terrified. He had let himself go too far and perhaps insulted Juan. He definitely was losing his head in the cell, but the capture of Felipe made him feel betrayed. He hated the casta divina and their friends in the military.

"Excuse me sir," Juan said in a quiet, high-pitched voice. "I am in the militia and I am with him. He is the best governor that Yucatan has ever had. He gave land to my family. He gave political rights to women. My own daughter is in school because of him, and she is thinking of a career in the government."

"Sorry, I am just having a hard time dealing with the fact that he is in jail. We need to find a way..."

"Do not worry, sir -- I have an idea. I am going to put something in the guards' food and put them to sleep. I just need to find more of one particular herb."

"Which herb is that?" Carlos asked, thinking this was a good idea. "Are you sure you don't want to buy a drug for that? I know a pharmacist who can help you."

"Oh, no, sir -- this herb is perfect for this. I will put it into the soup and then I will make some cigarettes for the guards to smoke to increase the effect."

"Where do you find it?"

"The name is zacatechichi and it is used by the Chantal Indians in Oaxaca to give a pleasant sleep. I once talked to a healer, a chilam, and he highly recommended it. This herb does not leave traces or give side effects, so I will be able to keep my job after Felipe Carrillo Puerto is gone. The only problem is that it does not cause a very deep sleep, so the guards could be awakened by loud noises."

I guess that is better that nothing, thought Carlos. "What about the keys?" he spoke aloud, thinking that the plan was full of holes.

"I have copies."

"How did you get them?"

"As I told you, I worked here for some time before the De La Huertistas arrived. In those days, we had only small-time criminals here, and the head of the guards trusted me with the keys to feed the prisoners. I made copies little by little throughout the year, thinking that one day, they might come in handy."

"You are a very resourceful fellow," Carlos said with a hint of happiness in his voice.

"What I really am is clumsy. I was worried that I would lose a key and get in a lot of trouble, and thought that having the copy at home would help me."

"Anyway, I am happy to have found you. When can we do this?" Carlos asked with urgency in his voice.

"I will start working on it right away, and don't worry, I will help you, too. When the time comes just walk straight out of the jail, try to make as little noise as possible, and disappear as fast as you can. Do not worry about everyone else. They will follow you."

"Thank you for everything you are doing," Carlos said.

"I am doing it for justice. I need to go now, as we have talked for a long time. I will try to keep in touch," Juan said, and his voice disappeared.

Carlos' hope surged, but he was worried that everything sounded too easy. Could the conversation be nothing more than an illusion, or could Juan be a fake, like the traditional Catrina, a skeleton dressed as a fancy lady ready to impress but in the end just a joke?

Carlos got in bed with a hopeful heart and silently wished good luck to this brave Juan who was taking such a heroic step. He slept deeply for the first time since arriving in jail, but woke up in the middle of the night with strange dreams in his head. He saw the widow Peon smiling at him, telling him in her high-pitched voice that she was coming back. In his dream, the old widow had more strength than Goliath and was unstoppable. And all the Mayan underworld gods, the Xibalba lords, were holding skeletons in their hands, supporting her like an army.

***

Felipe Carrillo Puerto was not far from Carlos. His handsome face did not hide his sadness, his normally impeccable shirt was wrinkled, and his brown eyes held a far-away look. He knew his imprisonment was unjust and he had high hopes that everything would turn out for the best.

Had something covered his eyes and prevented him from seeing the events that came so fast? People had tried to tell him that his enemies were moving with great speed and he knew that money was pouring from the hacienda owners to the corrupt army forces. But he never anticipated treason and betrayal. The Indians were now proud citizens, some working for the government and earning salaries for the first time in their lives. They would not turn their backs on the governor who helped them achieve so much.

President Obregon had seemed strong and secure in Mexico City. Who would have thought that De La Huerta would rebel? But rebel he did, beginning in Veracruz few months ago. In fact, he had asked Felipe to join him, but instead Felipe had confirmed his alliance with Obregon and sent to the United States for arms that had not arrived in time.

Still, Felipe had felt secure. He might be lacking in arms, but he had the people, his Indians. Little did he know that his own militia was turning on him. He supposed he could not blame them. If what he was hearing was right, the landowners were paying soldiers large bonuses to switch sides, a great deal of money for people who lived on beans and tortillas.

December had been a terrible month. In fighting the rebels, Felipe had divided his forces, sending help to Quintana Roo. While they were victorious there, something drastic changed as they returned. His reports said that the army left the train at a stop for drinks cheering "Viva Felipe Carrillo Puerto" and came back cheering "Viva De La Huerta." After that, it was just a matter of escape.

Felipe needed more time to turn around the situation. Through his lawyer, he was offering large payments for the liberation of himself and his friends. His captors had accepted the deal but it was difficult to trust the new military people in charge. The money needed to be ready the moment the liberation papers were signed.

Felipe sighed. His socialist state was not ready for another war. On the contrary, it was ready for a peaceful, prosperous future. His programs were starting to work. He was sick of the violence in his country, even if it had mostly missed Merida. In his last days in power, he had had people guarding him all the time, for the first time in his political career. He had hated that.

Felipe had been leading a prosperous state that was responding to his innovative ideas, he had had the president's support, and he had had Alma.

Felipe missed Alma painfully; she was his companion and comfort, the person with whom he wanted to share his success. He had looked forward to a full long life with her in peace, not the struggles of these times of war. She was a smart woman, great in conversation and possessing a soft point of view that always helped Felipe. She was also very pretty, and just thinking about her gave Felipe a knot in his stomach. She made him feel young.

His Pixal Halal, as he liked to call Alma, was suffering too. She had not been in Merida when he ran away, so at least she was safe. Felipe had sent Alma many letters since his imprisonment, but he doubted that she was getting any.

His lawyer had told him that the soldiers took Felipe's letters every time the lawyer left the jail with a handful, assuring him they would send them. But nobody had received any yet.

Now, each time that Felipe went to a different room of the prison he would try to hide letters to Alma in the sofas and chairs in the hope that maybe some cleaning person would find them and send them in secret. They were passionate letters to Alma, perhaps inappropriate, but he was getting desperate.

One day he was surprised to hear music coming from outside his cell. It was "Peregrina," Alma's song. The guards were doing this as a joke. Felipe felt humiliated at first, but then every time they played the song it made him feel closer to Alma. He remembered her face and her white body, his hands on her. And for the first time, he cried.

***

The next several days went by without Carlos speaking again with Juan, who came every day at the same time, but was always surrounded by soldiers.

Carlos noticed that there were more people in the prison. Soldiers constantly walked in and out of the courtyard, but now it seemed they were not all from Merida. He could see a variety of colors and races, from the small, dark Indian to the blond, blue-eyed creoles. The soldiers made nasty jokes to Felipe, and they played "Peregrina" for hours outside his jail cell, especially on the day that he was supposed to get married.

Carlos was thankful for the opportunity of having talked with Juan and recalled the conversation repeatedly, imagining Felipe Puerto escaping soon and having a happy reunion in Cuba or San Francisco or wherever Alma was living safely.

It was a dark night on what Carlos thought was January 4. Carlos was waiting for Juan to show up, though he had been absent for the past several days. Carlos was worried. There was sound in the area of the jail outside his cell, but he could not tell what was happening.

Without warning, his cell door opened, but no one came in. The door opened just an inch and stopped, and Carlos thought he could hear quiet steps running away.

He ventured a step out his cell door, but saw no one. All the lights were off and it was hard to see. He turned both ways. At one end of the corridor was a closed door, which Carlos knew from his past interviews led into a hallway and then to the main offices of the building. At the other end was a door that was half-open. Carlos did not know where that door led, but opted to use it.

He went through the door and ran down a set of stairs that took him to the main kitchen. He encountered no guards. Carlos was sweating hard and could feel the palpitations in his heart.

Once in the kitchen it was easy to choose the way. One of the doors was open directly to the back streets of the neighborhood. As he ran out, the smell of the kitchen stayed with him, the dirty, greasy smell of jail pursuing him on his way to freedom. As Juan had instructed, he never looked back. Carlos jumped on a horse that waited for him in the narrow street and hurried away.

When he was far away from the jail, he thanked this stranger, Juan, who had risked his life. He would be sure to tell Felipe about him and make him a hero.

Chapter 7:Huevos Motuleños (Motul-style Eggs)

Merida, 1923

Ingredients:

2 eggs

2 tortillas

¼ cup of ham cut in small cubes

3 tomatoes

1 clove of garlic

½ onion

1 cup of cooked peas

1 cup of cheese

½ cup of refried beans

Salt to taste

Fry the eggs sunny side up and place them on top of a tortilla spread with refried beans. Cover with the second tortilla. Blend the garlic, onion and tomatoes and reduce it to a heavy salsa. Cover the eggs and tortilla with the tomato salsa and finish with the ham, peas and the cheese.

Food is the surest way to someone's heart.

Amanda was in her room, alone. The swinging of the hammock she often used instead of her bed was monotonous and lazy. One of her feet hung from the hammock, occasionally pushing against a floor that felt cold to the touch. The rest of her body was wrapped in the beautiful hand-made hammock so that it looked like a cocoon with a butterfly ready to emerge.

She was sad, distressed. She felt that life was spinning out of control. The normally festive holiday season was passing almost without notice in the Diaz household.

Cacho was physically much better. Her back was healing fast and she was now walking and eating normally. But she was gone -- no longer Amanda's friend. The first days after Cacho had been attacked, Amanda had stayed in her room. In that time and since, Cacho never said a word to her. Amanda would hug Cacho and beg her to speak, but Cacho would only glance at her and turn her face the other way. Was Amanda guilty in what had happened to her?

Amanda felt it was unfair that Cacho was blaming her and had a pain in her heart that made it almost impossible to breathe. Cacho was like her sister. She had always been a part of the family, and the two girls had grown up together. In any case, it was her father, not Amanda, who had sent Cacho to work for that woman. If anyone was guilty, it was he.

But would a situation like this happen to her sister, or any girl from Amanda's class? Of course not. Cacho had for years worked at the house, though Amanda had often helped her to finish early so they could play. They went to different schools. Though it did not happen in Amanda's house, in other people's houses the servants would not even eat the same food.

Amanda felt like a fool, a stupid doll who did not see through the situation. She had never talked to Cacho about how much she hated the segregation that occurred. Yet she went to all the houses where Cacho was not welcome, her father encouraging her to spend time with people her own age and of her own social class.

She thought that her family was modern, and was proud of it, but her father had sent Cacho to work for that witch, the Peon widow, treating Cacho like a possession. Her father knew what kind of person the widow was and knowing that, he let her go. Was her family guilty of minor class segregation or a kind of slavery?

All this time that Amanda had criticized the casta divina, Cacho must have felt that she was a hypocrite. Amanda's family was guilty of the same behaviors, but wrapped them in nice words, hugs and secrets. But Amanda would keep taking care of Cacho. She was determined to win back her love.

Shifting from one set of problems to another, Amanda thought about Felipe Carrillo Puerto. She could not believe that he was dead. The unfair trial had ended a few days ago. The execution was against a cemetery sidewall yesterday.

***

Later, when all this would become history, the people of Merida would build him a mausoleum near that wall, but now the only reminders were some holes in the wall and the tears of hundreds of people.

Alma Reed would outlive Felipe Carrillo Puerto by decades, but in the end, her ashes would lie next to him. Merida would have a passionate love story forever.

Alma would have the Mexican seed planted deep in her heart. The rest of her life, she would promote and give humanitarian help to Mexico and its people. She would open galleries where unknown Mexican photographers and painters would have the chance to introduce themselves. She would become a friend of the painter Jose Clemente Orozco and would support him as he began work in the United States, on his way to becoming one of the most renowned painters in Mexico and the world.

Alma would write several books about Yucatan, mostly on archeology, her passion. Mexico in return would give her "El Aguila Azteca," the highest decoration that could be awarded to a foreigner.

After her romance with Felipe, Alma would never marry. Every time that the song "Peregrina" is played anywhere in the world, it is like adding one more day to their life together.

***

De La Huerta, the coup leader based in Veracruz on the Gulf of Mexico, could not get arms and munitions from the United States and had to rely on Belize and British Honduras. He needed to move arms through Yucatan, and Felipe Carrillo Puerto was in his way. A state that was usually not very important in the tribulations of Mexican politics was for this unique time crucial for the opposition's success. It was all just politics for De La Huerta.

The illegal government charged Felipe with treason and inappropriate use of government money. The trial and charges were all false. It is said that even the soldiers who captured Felipe Carrillo Puerto shed tears the day injustice killed him.

***

Amanda thought about Carlos sitting in jail for nothing and the situation in Merida getting worse by the day. Everything was in chaos. Amanda's father had no way to help Carlos. And Amanda herself was sick of being treated like a child.

She fell asleep without noticing, for the first time forgetting to say good night to Cacho. The next morning she awoke early with the first light and jumped out of her hammock. She tied it in the special knot used in Merida, hung it on the wall to make space in the room, and ran to the kitchen.

Jovita sat at the table as always, working. She was cleaning black beans, and the entire table was covered with a sheet of black dots as she was picking out small stones and little pieces of wood.

"Good morning," said Amanda.

"Good morning," said Jovita, and a strange looked crossed her face for a moment. She looked down to try to cover it.

"How is Cacho?" asked Amanda in her most concerned voice. She had not spoken much about the incident with Jovita and could not hide her shame. She felt the urge to kneel down and ask for forgiveness.

Jovita looked up and answered, "I am so sorry, Miss Amanda. I know you have been feeling badly about the situation, but I guess it is best that I just tell you straight out that Cacho is gone."

"Wait, wait, before you say something," continued Jovita. "She left of her own will and you need to respect that. She came to my room last night for advice. I gave her all the money that I had and my blessing. She is going to join Pedro in the United States." As if that were enough information, she went back to her picking job, now paying more attention to the task than before.

Amanda was tempted to hurl the table covered with beans against the wall, but she controlled herself. Jovita avoided Amanda's eyes, and Amanda just stood there watching Jovita work for what seemed a long time. Amanda knew that Jovita was very sad too, and finally decided to leave her alone, but not before giving her a long, silent hug.

Amanda thought that she could not feel any worse. She thought of these people as her family, and yet they did not include her in the decision. Maybe, after all these years, she was just the little white "owner" to them, someone to whom they would never feel attached. She left the room with her heart now completely broken.

Back in her room, she thought that the only thing left to do was to use all her energy to help get Carlos out of jail.

Not long after Amanda had this thought, a knock sounded on the front door. She heard someone open the door, and a crowd of soldiers rushed into the house and went to all the rooms without asking permission. The soldiers pulled Amanda's father and mother from their room. Amanda could hear the low, direct voice of her father demanding the reason for the intrusion.

The soldiers did not say a word. They just opened every door and looked into all possible hiding places. They left almost as fast as they had come.

Shortly after the last soldier left the house, one of the officers returned and said in a harsh voice, "Carlos Ancona has escaped from prison. If we find out that you or any of your family helped him at all, there will be more trouble than you can imagine." He left, closing the door with an incongruous gentleness, as if he finally realized that it was early in the morning and all civilized people were sleeping.

Amanda was shocked by the news. She was thrilled for Carlos, and this was the first good news she had heard in weeks. What would happen next? Would Carlos try to get in contact with the family, which would be a very dangerous situation? He would find a way, for sure. Would he come and ask her to run away with him? Was she ready for that? She imagined for the first time a life with him, and she was not sure if she would like it.

***

One day a few weeks later, Amanda awoke alone in her room. Her room was the same, her furniture was the same, her life was the same, but she was not the same. She cried a great deal. She sometimes stayed in her swinging hammock and cried with every swing, the sobs strung together like a song, day after day. The highlight of the day was when Jovita left breakfast outside her room with xtabentum flowers as decoration. What was the point anymore of getting up to do things? She had no friends and no boyfriend.

Carlos had not contacted them. She understood -- his life was in danger. It seemed that they did not know anything about anyone. Weeks had gone by without any news of either Carlos or Cacho. Amanda's family had retreated from the local politics, trying not to attract any attention. Her father spent much of his time alone in the living room, just reading. The only one who had kept her normal routine was Amanda's mother, always in her room. Perhaps Amanda was becoming her mother's child after all.

Today Amanda needed to get out of her room. She decided to wake up early and take a walk out in the yard. Sunrise had always been her favorite time of the day. It made her think with anticipation of the great things that the day would bring, but lately it seemed that she had nothing to look forward to. She walked outside, and the covered birdcages around the courtyard looked like ghosts waiting to haunt her.

She walked around for a half an hour and ended up leaning against a corner wall that was hidden away, the shrubbery making a little cave in which to sit. As the light began to brighten, Amanda sat still, enjoying the unique colors that a sunrise can bring.

After a few minutes, a white ghost appeared out of nowhere. The figure seemed to be floating across the grass, stopping here and there to smell some flowers. When the ghost was near enough, Amanda was surprised to recognize the ethereal figure of her mother in her white hipil. It made Amanda remember a time when she would secretly watch her mother, just in the hope of grasping some of her attention or sharing some moments with her.

Amanda noticed that her mother already had several flowers in her hand, and she knew at once which kind they were. She could smell vanilla and honey from where she sat.

Her mother carried a bunch of xtabentum flowers. Amanda's heart fluttered. Was it possible that all these years it had been her mother who had left these flowers outside her room? She then saw her mother going into the kitchen, and the noise that came from inside indicated that she was making breakfast. The smell of tomatoes and fried eggs wafted through the window. Huevos Motuleños. It was Amanda's favorite breakfast.

Amanda was in a state of shock, her entire body frozen. Little by little, a warm feeling grew in her, and she felt a small pressure in her heart. She cried again, but for the first time in a long time, it was from joy. She saw her mother come out of the kitchen with the food and the flowers all set up to leave outside her room. After leaving the breakfast, her mother walked back to her own room with silent steps and closed the door as quietly as she could.

Amanda left her hiding place and thought, why? Why did her mother never show her any affection? Why did she need to hide it from everyone? Amanda walked to her room and ate her breakfast with a strange pleasure. As she slowly put the pieces of food into her mouth, she imagined that each bite was a kiss from her mother. Food tasted better that day.

Amanda finished her food, and all that was left on the plate were the tears she had shed while she was eating. She looked at the flowers. As the story said, the flowers came from an exotic woman who did not fear life. Amanda needed some answers. She opened her bedroom door and ran to her mother's door, but she could not knock on the door. Amanda would not be able to confront her mother – all these years of not talking had built a wall between them. She barely knew the sound of her mother's voice. She decided to talk to her father instead.

Amanda went to look for her father in the living room, where she knew he was spending much of his time reading. She was not surprised to see him there peacefully reading a book in the perfect light of the early morning. The room was dark except for a shaft of light shining on her father's chair; it matched her mood perfectly.

Amanda held the xtabentum flower bouquet. Her father looked at her and saw a strange smile on her face, both happy and sad.

"Good morning Amanda. How are you?" he said, leaving the book he was reading on a side table.

"I found out where these flowers come from, Papi," Amanda said in a small voice.

"You are finally reading some of the Mayan folk stories, Amanda. I am happy for you," he said, smiling, and his warm eyes looked at her with knowledge of her new discovery. He stood up and went to hug her.

Amanda cried and cried for long time and her father stood there holding her until she was calmer. He guided the two of them to a sofa.

"Why, Papi, why? Why does my mother feel ashamed of her love for me? Right now, I don't know if it would be better to know that I was not loved or to know that someone loves me but does not want to show it. What have I done wrong?" Amanda looked at her hands as if she were the builder of the lie herself.

"Amanda, it is not you. It was never you. It is your mother and her pain and her ghosts," Amanda's father said, holding his daughter's chin with his gentle hands and looking deeply into her eyes.

"What ghosts? I don't understand."

"Amanda, there is a secret in this family that we have kept hidden from you and your sister for a long time. There are many reasons why we hid it from you, but listen to my story and try to understand your mother better than anyone else does. All right?" he asked.

"I'll try," Amanda said, trying to calm herself, but holding her father's hand more tightly.

"You know that your mother came from one of the wealthiest families in the region."

"Yes, I know. It is all that property that we never work and..."

"Amanda, please listen to my story and try not to interrupt until I finish. Okay?"

Amanda nodded gravely and decided to let her father talk freely. She had never seen her father this serious. She recognized the seriousness of the moment and began to feel frightened. She knew that after this conversation she was going to be another person, that she was going to become an adult. For the first time, her father was talking to her not as though she were a little girl. She was breaking the first window of her glass castle. She was ready.

"Your mother grew up in a rich family, but most of the money came from the side of her mother. Her mother's family owned a number of henequen haciendas, what people used to call "green money" haciendas, and your grandmother was the only child. The haciendas were productive and profitable at the time, not abandoned as are they now. But when your grandmother became a young woman, she married a politician who did not care for farm work."

"Oh yes, my grandfather. I know that he left my grandmother for another woman and went to live in Mexico

City. We never saw him though, even though Grandma never divorced him. Am I right?"

"Yes," her father said, putting a gentle finger in front of her mouth to remind her to keep quiet. "He moved to Mexico City and left your grandmother with 3 boys and a girl to raise. Money was not a problem. Your grandmother was the only child, and her father was alive and running the haciendas. They both trained your uncles in the henequen business. Your uncles were young, just teenagers, and your great-grandfather was an old-fashioned landlord."

"It was the years just before the Revolution, and social unhappiness was everywhere. Henequen workers were treated like slaves, even on the haciendas owned by your mother's family. Your uncles had just started to get involved in the process, but even they soon noticed the poor treatment of the workers. They were just becoming an age to understand more. What your uncles did not know was that the hacienda overseers hated them because they were young, because they were unknown, and mostly because they were the grandsons of the owner.

"In those days, each of the family's haciendas was run by an overseer. These overseers were masters of the land and the workers, and were treated like gods on the haciendas. Needless to say, they were very happy with the status quo. But as your uncles grew to better understanding of the business, they began to realize that the overseers were corrupt. A careful review of the books showed that a number of the overseers were stealing money from the family. During this time, your great-grandfather died of old age, leaving the haciendas to your grandmother. Since your uncles were still young and your mother younger still, they did not inherit directly. Still, there was money for everyone, even if far less than the haciendas should have been yielding.

"As your uncles became men, they went to live on the haciendas and took a more active role in management. They wanted to change the industry, starting a model that would properly compensate workers and provide them better living conditions. They knew that this was a process that would take years, but they were young and idealistic. A first step was buying out the overseers and replacing them with new ones they could trust. Then they would provide better lives for the workers. But this would take money, more than they or your grandmother could easily raise.

"By this time your mother and I were married, Julieta had been born, and your mother was seven months pregnant with you. Your uncles' first step after your grandmother was to contact us looking for a loan, but I was just starting my import company and did not have the cash. The only person who could lend them that kind of money was their absent father. Since her brothers could not leave the haciendas, your mother decided to go to Mexico City and ask her father for the money.

"I had just ordered a large shipment of Serrano hams and needed to be there when they arrived from Spain. I wanted Norma to wait until after you were born, but her brothers made the situation sound urgent, and she did not want to waste time. Plus, she said that she was feeling great. I believed her, and reluctantly agreed to the trip.

"Your mother traveled by train, over my objections. She had always been a strong woman. Strong in her head, too," Amanda's father said, smiling a little.

"Pre-Revolution unrest had begun, and it was an odyssey to get to Mexico City. A number of strikes delayed her journey, but at last, she arrived.

"Your grandfather knew she was coming and was at the train station waiting for her with a large bouquet of flowers and his charming personality. He took her to his big house outside Mexico City in what is now called Parque Lira, where he lived with his mistress and her two children. Your mother accused him of abandoning them and never looking back. He argued that as a liberal thinker he could not live a life married to a member of the class that was the cause of the social unrest. It's true, your grandmother was a true member of the casta divina, with the bluest blue blood of all. But, after several days of family guilt and fighting, your grandfather gave Norma the money.

"During these days, the whole story came out. Your grandfather had fallen desperately in love with your grandmother at a very young age. They worked hard at being happy for several years, but her family, the old landowners, pushed him and humiliated him as being somehow less than worthy of their daughter. Your grandfather began to believe them. Your grandmother was an only child. She was close to her parents and would never side against them. They fought more and more until he finally left Merida and moved to Mexico City. Divorce was out of the question, and he was happy that he eventually found someone who accepted him without the prospect of marriage.

"After she had heard his side of the story, Norma reconciled with her father. She accepted him for what he was. It was easier to love than to hate.

"Your mother came back to Merida, now nine months pregnant but with a happy smile and a suitcase full of money. The money was ready for me to take to your uncles, but the morning that I was to leave, your mother went into labor. You were ready to be born.

"I could not leave your mother in labor. She had had a very dangerous delivery with Julieta, and almost died. So I stayed home.

"Later that day, we heard news from the haciendas. A band of rebels had gone through and destroyed the haciendas where your uncles lived. They had killed everyone. I would have been killed too, if not for the timing of your birth.

"Your mother was devastated. She cried and screamed against the rebels. She was angry at the injustice of life. The rebels could have chosen any haciendas to destroy, but they chose those of Norma's brothers.

"Two hours later, a new face appeared at our door. A man introduced himself as one of the new overseers about to be hired by your uncles. He told us a completely different story, that your three uncles had been murdered by the old hacienda overseers. While the terrified man hid in the jungle, he saw how, one by one, the overseers used their machetes to hack your uncles' bodies countless times. The overseers had learned of your uncles' plans to replace them and used the rebel situation to cover the murders.

"It was then that your mother changed. For days, she seemed out of her mind. She had in her hands the money that could have changed her brothers' lives, but had been unable to use it in time. You were born in the midst of this, hours after that terrible news arrived. You came into the world, but part of your mother's soul died that day. She never recovered that light she always had in her eyes. She still hates herself for her delay, and thinks that she wasted valuable time with her father in Mexico City, selfishly trying to get to know him while her brothers were in danger.

"Now, every time she comes out of her room, she sees everyone as an enemy. She wants to blame the Indians, the workers at the hacienda, the help in the houses, anyone who stood there without helping, the transportation workers whose strikes delayed her trip. She has so much hate in her heart that it consumes her. She thinks that she needs to stay in her room to cleanse herself of bad thoughts. On top of that, you look like one of her brothers, so every time she sees you she is reminded of her sorrow. Deep down she is still a good person, and knows that you deserve better. But she cannot forgive herself or the others, and the only thing for me to do is accept the circumstances and wait for the day when she gets better."

"Oh, Papi, I am so sorry," Amanda said, hugging him.

"Don't be sorry. I am a happy man. I have you and your sister, and for me that's more than enough. And I know that one day I am going to get back your mother." He said this with a gentle smile and returned Amanda's hug, along with a kiss to her cheek. They kept each other company for a while as the house came alive as always.

Later, Amanda was back in her room. The story that she had just heard was incredible. Why do people keep these secrets in their lives? Parents always want to protect their children, but sometimes the secrets hurt more than the truth. She wished that someone had told her the story earlier. She had grown up thinking that her mother did not love her, and this left her confused about love because she was missing the most important type, the love of a mother. Now she knew that in reality the tragedy was not about her, that she was secretly loved by her mother. But her mother was paying for her imaginary sins in her own way.

Amanda thought about her life and felt a kinship to her mother. She, too, was secluding herself inside a room for no good reason. Nothing had happened to her. She had not made a difference in anyone's life. She realized that she wanted to make a difference for someone and that someone was Cacho. Cacho needed her. Amanda thought about their life growing up together and determined that she and Cacho would fulfill one of the dreams they shared when there were young and hiding notes under the courtyard tree.

They both had wanted to go to school, study, and be professional women. Once they met Alma Reed, they wanted to be writers or journalists, but when they were young, they switched every year between being a teacher, a nurse, and maybe if luck was on their side, a doctor or a lawyer. They were young and did not know how hard was for a woman in Mexico to be a doctor or lawyer, but now Amanda wanted to take that challenge and make something happen.

She knew of schools in the United States that would take foreigners. She was going to ask her father if she could study abroad, and on her way to the college, she would find Cacho and take her along.

Amanda was sure that if Cacho were in the United States she would contact Alma Reed for help, so Amanda would start her search there. She would take along all of Cacho's papers, so both could enroll at the same school, and both would have the same opportunities. This would make them real sisters.

Amanda was so excited that she started going through her closet choosing the things to take. It was getting dark and the day was gone, but she realized that this had been the most productive day of her life.

She lay in her hammock and realized that she had one last task to do before going to sleep.

It was dark when Amanda left her room, but she knew her way and the moon was bright. She carried scissors from her room and found the right bushes within minutes. She cut dozens of xtabentum flowers, carried them back into the house, and piled them in front of her mother's room. She was making up for lost years. The aroma of vanilla and honey was so strong in the hallway that the birds in their covered cages woke up with the smell. It was strange to hear the birds at night. It was as if finally their ghosts were waking up and leaving the house for good. The song was a fanfare to the beginning of her new life and the end of a sad nightmare. The sound was chasing out the fog that hid behind the furniture and between the sheets of the beds.

She was just closing the door to her room when she saw her mother coming out of her own door. Norma was surprised at first, but soon turned toward Amanda's door. Their eyes met, and for the first time in her life, Amanda felt the love that she always wanted coming from her mother's eyes, which then filled with tears. Amanda expected her mother to come over and embrace her, but instead she stepped back into her room and closed the door behind her.

Amanda did not mind, for what she had just experienced was enough for now. It would take time and patience to start their relationship, but now she knew that she was on the right track and that her mother wanted to change it, too.

Chapter 8: Cenotes

Merida, 1985-1986

Cenote: A natural fresh water well. A gift from the gods.

- Mayan thought

Hope and dreams run through lives like water in underground rivers. Knowing that deep inside there is always water makes a person relax, a bit like having life insurance.

The time after my grandmother's funeral had been the saddest of my life. But soon, it was time to say goodbye to my family and Mexico City and return to Chicago. The parting at the airport left me with watery eyes, a shrinking heart, and a hollow stomach for the flight to my adopted home.

I was soon back to my normal life focused on the kids, school, food and the unfinished list of household chores that had piled up in my absence. I made a point, though, to dedicate at least half a morning each week to investigating the documents I had found.

The only real clue that I had was the name Villanueva. I looked in the phone book and found over 50 people in Chicago (which has a Hispanic population of hundreds of thousands) with that name. I took the list and began calling the numbers, most often leaving messages at first, but eventually connecting with someone at each house. No one had any familiarity with my story or any ideas to help me. After several months of calling, I finished the list with no answers.

I felt like I was going into a black cave with only one match. This made me think of the black hole in the story of my grandmother's life, the part about which we knew little: her time in Merida.

Winter break was approaching, and my husband and I decided to take the kids and head to Yucatan. Merida is a much smaller city than Chicago, so perhaps it would be easier to learn about my grandmother's family or even find someone who would recognize the men in the photo.

That December, we arrived in Merida, the beautiful capital of the state of Yucatan. This was an exciting trip: a week in Merida, followed by three days in Cancun, then a trip down to Playa del Carmen, where we would take the ferry to Cozumel for a New Year's Eve celebration at a relative's house on the beach.

Merida welcomed us with moderate, warm weather, very comfortable in the winter. We knew that some relative would pick us at the airport, but I was surprised to see my cousin Mauricio, who had grown two feet since the last time I saw him and was driving his girlfriend's van. We all loaded into the van, using every available inch for bags and presents. The loud air conditioning made it difficult to have any kind of conversation, so I focused my attention on the road and on the exotic views.

As we left the airport, we entered the jungle that surrounds Merida. It was like a solid wall of green being eaten little by little by the road as we drove through. It looked as if a gardener had cut all the trees the same height. Not too tall, perfect for the Mayan people who had lived in this jungle for millennia.

The outskirts of the city showed the normal signs of recent growth -- American fast food chains, car dealers and broad, straight streets.

The land was so flat that we had unobstructed views down the long streets into the residential parts of the city. House walls ended at the curbs without yards in front. Parked cars lined both sides of the streets, leaving narrow lanes to let traffic pass. It felt crowded, but also fine, rich, and full of stories. People in the streets looked happy and unhurried, and many stood outside their open doors talking with neighbors, their lack of concern with security reflecting the safety of the city.

My father and my aunt waited for us at the hotel, having arrived earlier on their drive from Mexico City. My father said that he wanted to drive so he could stop in couple of cities along the way, but the real reason was that we needed a big car to transport all the people, and my father felt useful being the one driving for his family. My father drove a Suburban, which can seat nine people. He had enjoyed every minute of the drive, stopping in Puebla for chiles en nogada and in Valladolid for longaniza, arguing that all regional foods taste much better in their place of origin.

Another reason from them to drive was shopping. They liked to stop along the way and buy authentic furniture or pottery from the indigenous people. My aunt was most interested in buying recados, salty pastes made with different spices that are used for cooking Yucatan dishes. Merida has a great variety of the fragrant concoctions, which can only be found in the central market of the city, where the same families that have made them for generations still sell them.

I love one special recado dish named *papat-zules*, "the king's dish," which is made with a green paste of pumpkin seeds, soaked in herbs and made into the salsa for a delicious, egg-filled taco.

We were staying at the Fiesta Americana Hotel at the end of El Paseo Monetejo, the street called by locals "The Champs Elysees of Merida." I could not wait to show my husband and children the street's beautiful houses, built when Merida was one of the richest cities in Mexico, back when my grandmother was a teenager and henequen was as good as gold, green gold.

I do not know if it is a Mexican tradition or just a family tradition, but the first thing that everyone wanted to do was eat. Moreover, the first thing that must be eaten in Merida is tacos of cochinita pibil. Not surprisingly, just a block from the hotel was a restaurant serving these tacos all day long.

We crowded into the restaurant with empty stomachs and large appetites. The tacos were delicious, pork cooked in an orange annatto salsa tinged with deep red-brown flecks. The tables had all the usual toppings in the center: a good habanero salsa and onions cooked with bay leave and vinegar. To wash down our food, we all drank glasses of horchata, a white rice drink flavored with cinnamon.

Back on the street to our hotel, we walked past the bust of a man named Eligio Ancona, who in the 1870s had been governor of Yucatan and was a well-known writer of colonial Yucatan history. We decided to take our first official photograph of the trip. I was happy to try out my new camera.

This was not my first visit to Merida, called by Mexicans "the white city." I had been there as a little girl with my grandmother and my aunt. The people we visited all seemed to live in big houses with high ceilings (perfect for the intense heat), adjoined by big yards and courtyards where a young girl could safely get lost. But the main thing I remember from that trip was all the family that I had never before met. They were excited to see me, and showered me with endless hugs and wet kisses on the cheek, which of course I hated.

My second trip was a summer during university. One of my "uncles" (actually a second cousin once removed, or something like that) had rented a house for the summer on a beach near Progreso, and a school friend and I stayed there for two weeks. We slept in hammocks, swam in the sea, and at night looked for crabs. Everything was so unspoiled. I remember how the crabs made little holes in the sand in which to hide, and after the waves covered them with water, the crabs spouted bubbles to clear the holes. There were thousands of those little holes on the beachfront, so many that we could not avoid stepping on them. As we looked back at our footprints, we felt like giants.

Because the summertime heat in inland Merida is so intense, everyone who can afford to moves to the coast for a few months. They improvise discos and bars with sand floors and fire pits to light the night and the romance. My friend and I met a few guys from Merida, but strangely enough, we were considered too old to be dating. Many Merida girls of our age were already engaged or married. We were university students! We were not close to getting married, and had no desire to.

After living my whole life to that point in Mexico City, it was funny to live in a small town for a change, where everyone knew each other. It was amusing to see how they would ask for our entire names, trying to understand how we were connected. They accepted us, but it made me sometimes want to say my name was K'anlol, a flower in Mayan, just for fun.

The food was excellent, especially the fresh fish caught by local fishermen, the delicious licorice-flavored breads that accompanied our dinners, and the tasty Mexican orange cheddar cheese, similar to American cheese but not very popular in Mexico City at that time.

One special night, we went to a dinner party at the home of one of my uncle's friends, who turned out to have known my grandmother when she was young and had many photographs of my grandmother as a young woman. She had been so pretty.

Our hostes's memorabilia included several of the little dancecards that girls of that time used at parties to dance with boys. All the songs that the band was planning to play were listed, each with a blank line next to it that the dancers needed to fill in to share a song. Many of the songs were scratched out, which our hostess explained meant that the girl was reserving those songs for her favorite boy of the evening.

Looking at the dancecards with accompanying photos of young ladies all dressed according to the theme of that particular party, I realized that I knew very little about my grandmother's life as a young woman. I interrupted our hostes's explanation of the details of a "blue and white" party to ask if my grandmother ever went to parties like that.

"Your grandmother moved to the United States and missed all the fun," was her answer. But before I could ask what she meant, we were interrupted by the sounds of loud singing and one of the guests tugging at the hostes's elbow and asking her to go out to the beach.

There was a bonfire on the beach and two guitars came out. We ended up spending the rest of the night singing the old bohemian songs full of love and passion that I had learned from my family growing up.

My other main memory from that trip to the beach is how bad the mosquitoes were, like an army that I never knew existed. Where I grew up in Mexico City, above 7,000 feet elevation, we almost never saw mosquitoes. But in Progreso, we had to keep our bedrooms sealed day and night and spray for insects each day. Still, the little bloodsuckers would find a way to us somehow. One night we failed to make sure that the windows were perfectly closed and woke the next day looking like we had chicken pox. I felt utterly defeated by Mother Nature.

I felt the same way years later when I first moved to Chicago and struggled to survive my first winter. It was like some monster, but I finally realized that I had to relax and get used to it, because it would always be there.

That trip as a young woman opened my eyes, especially to the fact that my grandmother's family was very prominent in Merida, which made it even more strange how little she talked about her social life growing up there. It sounded like so much fun. But now I know why. She was hiding a big secret, and the less contact that we had with the people who knew her when she was young, the better she liked it.

After that trip, I tried to get more information and stories from her but she never said anything relevant to my current search. She said that they were old stories that were better off forgotten, and always redirected the topic to a funny story from her life in Mexico City, trying to make me lose my initial train of thought.

This trip to Merida was different. I had a mission to get more information about my grandmother and her family. All my life, whenever anyone had asked why she had left Merida she told the story about being diagnosed with tuberculosis. She said that the doctor had forbidden her to stay in Merida because the extreme heat would complicate her weak health. I was not yet sure how I would do it (the old friend I had met on my last trip had passed away), but I was determined to learn more.

That afternoon we walked down the Paseo Montejo, the street where many of the *Casta Divina* had lived in the days of my grandmother's youth. I was happy to see that most of the grand old mansions were in great shape, though many had been converted to house banks, insurance companies or upscale restaurants. They looked so beautiful, and seeing them made me believe it when people said that at beginning of the 20th century Merida had more millionaires than any other city in the world.

Our final destination was the Colon ice cream shop, something I knew my kids would like. We tried a wide variety of special fruit flavors, and as we sat there, I noted from a sign that the ice cream parlor had been open since 1907, just a year after my grandmother was born. I realized I was getting a little too obsessive, and decided to enjoy the rest of the day and not think about the past until tomorrow.

After breakfast the next morning, the entire family took taxis to the historical center of Merida, knowing that we would not be able to park a car as large as the Suburban on the narrow streets common in Mexican colonial cities. Merida's city center is charming and a great place to spend a day. The kids particularly loved the variety of balloons sold by a man in a palm hat and white outfit, standing next to a vendor of bouncing balls and colorful pinwheels. We visited all the important monuments, including the cathedral (quite somber compared with those in other Mexican colonial cities) and the Montejo house, the residence of Merida's founder.

After the last landmark and a late lunch, we decided to find the house in which my grandmother had grown up. My aunt knew that the house had been converted into a school and was behind the Mother's Park, one block from the zocalo, or central plaza, of Merida.

It is easy to move around in Merida, as the streets are laid out in a grid, like an American city. We found the Mother's Park easily enough, and were welcomed by the sights of artists selling their paintings, a beautiful statue of a Madonna and Child, and a theater and a church bordering the gardens. And there, across the street, was the school that had once been a house.

The front of the house was like most other houses in Merida, with no yard in front, the walls of the house coming right up to the street, and a few large windows protected and decorated by iron bars in the typical Mexican style. The door that had once been wood was now an iron monster with a large sign promoting the school.

I had stayed in houses like this before and knew that if you are sitting in the front room, even with the windows closed, it is easy to listen many of the conversations on the street, which is great for the spread of small-town gossip.

We knocked on the great door of my grandmother's house several times, and then rang the bell repeatedly. Just when we thought that no one would come, a loud metallic noise came from inside and the door swung open. A tall, thin, sleepy-looking fellow came out wearing a straw hat. It took him a moment to adjust to the brilliant afternoon light, but then he said in a harsh voice, "What do you want? The school is closed! Come back later."

He was about to close the door when my father said, "Wait, wait. We are not here for the school. I think I was born here."

As the man absorbed that information, I snuck a bill into his hand.

"Listen," I said. "We have just come from Mexico City, and this used to be the house of our relatives. Is there any way that we can just have a quick look around?"

He pocketed the bill, looked at me, and smiled. "Okay, but just for a second. Don't take too long; I have things to do."

Like sleeping, I thought, realizing that it was siesta time. We were all used to Mexico City, where no one takes siestas any more. But in the provinces, in particular where the weather is very hot, the tradition of after-lunch siestas is alive and well. I remember how proudly my grandmother used to tell us that when she lived here she liked to play chess with her father while the rest of the house was sleeping away the afternoon in an attempt to avoid the blazing heat and the tropical sun.

We went into the house and made our way to the central courtyard. Everything was white.

"Hey," my father said, pointing to a tile floor that had an inlay of darker tiles around the outside, "I remember this floor. I used the dark tiles as the streets for my toy cars. Wow! It is unbelievable how things come back." He laughed.

Unfortunately, there was not much more to see. The courtyard was a simple concrete patio and the walls of the empty halls had some students' work on them. The classrooms that we guessed used to be bedrooms were small for their current purposes, but big for sleeping chambers.

"There is a second patio," my father said. "I remember because my favorite place, the kitchen, was there. I used to run there to eat fresh-made tortillas with salt."

"You are right, sir," the caretaker said. "There is a second patio at the back of the school. It is used by some of the grades for their recess."

"Can we go?" my father and I asked at the same time.

"The way to get there is through that door," he said, pointing to a large metal door on the right side of the courtyard. "That provides access to the principal's office, and it is closed and locked. Sorry."

"No problem," I said. We were just happy to be there. The building was very large for a house and from what we could see the layout did not appear to have been changed through remodeling. But my father could not remember which rooms had been used for what purposes. He was very young when he moved away to Mexico City.

Before we left, I took out the photograph that we had found in my grandmother's closet and showed it to the caretaker.

"Have you taken care of this house for a long time?" I asked. "Do you recognize any of these people?"

"Sorry, but no. I work for the school and came when it opened." When I let out a sad sigh, he continued, "But, I know that the old caretaker's family bought the convenience store on the corner and is still there. You can go and ask them, guapa." The caretaker finished with a smile.

A few minutes later, we were at the store. It was a typical corner store, with the small space dominated by a pair of refrigerators full of Coca-Cola products and a wall covered with delicious potato chips. Colorful candies and round packages of gum were on display on top of the counter.

All this junk food was too much for my kids and me. There is something about the chips in Mexico that makes them taste much better than those in the U.S. We bought potato chips with lime, popcorn with chile powder, habanero chips, orange and cinnamon cookies, and five or six different drinks. My kids were happy and the owner was too, if his broad smile could be trusted. It was a good way to introduce ourselves.

I asked my husband to take the kids back to the hotel because I was beginning to think that this was going to take a long time. The owner had seen the photograph and asked us to sit down while he finished taking care of some customers.

"Sorry to keep you waiting, preciosa," he said with a smile. I was beginning to enjoy the Yucatan custom of calling people "precious" or "beautiful." Maybe we should all do that more often.

"I think I know who these people are. They were the Diaz girls, daughters of Don Aurelio Diaz," he said, looking into my eyes.

I returned his look, pausing to control my eagerness. He was so short that I was looking down, which is a bit of a miracle because I am not a tall person. He had dark skin, brown eyes, and a very round face.

He was wearing a typical guayabera, the traditional dress shirt for men of the region, made of cotton and distinguished by having numerous pockets on the front, including some down near the waist. As has long been the custom in the region, he had this shirt outside his pants, a look that worked because the shirt has an even bottom, not the tails of other dress shirts.

He would probably be surprised to learn that he looked very fashionable; in the United States, this type of shirt and un-tucked look was in. Hollywood stars were using guayaberas, but with many different colors and textures. I guessed that some fashion guru had spent a summer in Merida.

"One is our grandmother, Amanda, and the other, the blond one, is her sister, Julieta," my sister said. We still could not get over how different the two of them looked at such a young age.

"Oh, the Diaz daughters were well known to be beautiful," he replied.

"Do you happen to know the two men in the photo?" I asked.

"Well," he said, holding out the photograph, "this guy looks like Gualberto Carrillo Puerto, the brother of a former governor. I am not completely sure but he does look like him. The other guy, I don't know. Sorry." With that, he gave back the photograph and moved to take care of a new customer who had entered the store.

We were happy. We had learned a new name and had something to investigate. We were about to leave when the owner spoke up again.

"Maybe you should go and visit Ramona. As a girl, she worked for the Diaz family, and when they sold the house, they bought her a little house in Progreso. She used to come to visit me, but now she is pretty old."

We had a second name, and of a living person: Ramona. This was great fun, interesting and exciting. Tomorrow, we would look for Ramona.

We returned to our hotel happy. On our way, we stopped at a bookstore and found a biography of Felipe Carrillo Puerto. The identification was complete. There was a photograph of the Carrillo Puerto brothers in the middle of the book, and there was no doubt that one of the men in our photo was Gualberto Carrillo Puerto. Was he our relative? None one of us looked at all like him or any of his family, plus he was from a very prominent and known family at the time. In a little town like Merida, the secret or story of the illicit offspring of the governor's brother would never have stayed hidden. He also looked too old for my grandmother, and it all just did not seem to fit.

That night, I stayed awake reading the history book. I arrived at the conclusion that it was almost impossible for Gualberto Carrillo be our ancestor. At the time of his death, he was married with children. Plus, the book said that a firing squad had killed him on January 3, 1924, after he had spent a month between the jail and the jungle. The birth certificate from the closet said that my father was born on September 26, which meant that my grandmother likely conceived at the beginning of January or end of December, while Gualberto was on the run or in jail.

My grandmother never talked much about my father when he was a baby, but I remembered that she did mention the he was a big baby. My father liked to eat, and she would say that he was born big with plenty of room to distribute the food. She never mentioned that he was a premature baby.

I just did not see my grandmother being involved with Gualberto Carrillo Puerto. This whole process was subject to imagination, but I felt I needed to follow my instincts, and they said to follow the other man, the one with bright eyes and a sincere smile.

There was another clue in the photograph that could also be important. Someone had written "Love, Alma" on the back in English, and it made me wonder if this Alma could be Alma Reed, the fiancée of Felipe Carrillo Puerto. This was getting better! It looked like our relatives were in the middle of one the most famous of Yucatan love tragedies.

Thinking back that night on our visit to my grandmother's house, it seemed like a different world. A large house full of servants hosting fancy dinners and parties felt unreal. It was funny how cosmopolitan the situation looked, and how normal it all was for the people who talked about it, as if Merida were Paris or New York.

The city was still pretty and some of the houses were as grand as any back home in the suburbs of Chicago, but few of them were still private residences. I guess it is easy for a city to change. It is sad to see world-class cities fall from grace. Some, like Havana and Beirut, suffer because of conflict and war. In the case of Merida, it was the invention of a less-expensive fiber to replace the natural fibers from henequen.

One of the most charming aspects of Merida was the way many people used traditional forms of dress on the streets in their everyday activities. They were proud of their heritage here, from both Europe and the indigenous people.

No one had conquered the Mayans as the Spaniards had conquered the Aztecs. The impressive Mayan civilization was gone when the Spanish arrived, and instead Yucatan had many small towns without any central power. People in all the towns spoke Mayan. They still speak Mayan today. They are walking reminders of their ancient cities and civilization, testaments to their magnificence; they would survive centuries, hidden but proud. The people of Yucatan had incorporated many Mayan words into their Spanish dialect, and some children of wealthy families grew up knowing Mayan better than Spanish because of their babysitters. My own grandmother once told me that she could understand Mayan perfectly.

In Mexico City, one does not see as much traditional garb as in Merida. Poor women who beg on the street corners use traditional long skirts, huaraches, or sandals, and *rebozos*, long, strong pieces of colorful material in which they carry their small children while begging (or at least something they want people to think of as small children). Someone once told me that "the Marias," as locals called these women, do not dress like that every day. They don these outfits as costumes to get more money. It works for me, if that is true, because every time I see a woman like that I cannot stop myself from giving money.

The hipiles in Merida are another story. They are important and treasured because many times they are hand made by the owners, incorporating favorite colors and types of flowers. The hipiles show lineage and personality. Women show their marital status. A married woman will use a blouse and a skirt; an unmarried one will wear an extra underskirt. Status and money show through accessorizing with golden earrings and necklaces. The workmanship on the dress is important too, especially the quality of the cross-stitching that goes into the floral patterns.

My grandmother talked about these things when she was alive. I even had a small hipil that I wore when I was a girl of five or six. Now I wished I had paid more attention to my grandmother or had a better memory, so I could explain these things to my own children.

I decided to buy hipiles for myself and for my daughter. It brings a smile to my face every time that I see a woman on the street wearing one. That could be us; it would remind us of this fun trip and perhaps bring a smile to someone else.

The next morning, we left early. It was to be a fun day for the kids because I had promised a trip to the beach and maybe a swim in a natural swimming hole or well. My family was excited.

Cenotes are the water wells of Yucatan. They are very important and beautiful, and for a long time were the only places to get fresh water. The Yucatan peninsula is made of limestone, and surface water filters down through it. There are no surface rivers or lakes on the peninsula, but water does flow underground. Where cave-ins have exposed parts of those subterranean rivers we have cenotes, with water some distance below the surrounding land.

We decided to visit Xcalah, a cenote north of Merida on the way to Progreso. I knew that it was not the most beautiful cenote, but it was close to the city, open to swimming, and near some Mayan ruins that could be visited. It was also a national park, which meant it would have bathrooms, important when traveling with children. On the way, I tried to attract my kids' attention by telling stories about cenotes.

"How far from the swimming pool are we?" my impatient young Joseph asked, his face turned to the window, worrying me that he would get carsick and ruin the trip.

"We are close. How are you feeling?" I asked, looking back at them and feeling guilty about their bored faces.

"Good," they both said, which was very fortunate, as my husband, Carl, struggled to follow the bad signs on the even-worse "highway."

"You know, the cenotes were also religious places," Carl said, looking for something to occupy their attention. "Joseph called it a swimming pool, but cenotes are really fresh-water wells, parts of rivers. Because this part of Yucatan is hot and usually dry, the cenotes were so important to the Mayan people that they tied their important religious ceremonies to them."

"On the History Channel I learned that some Mexican Indians did human sacrifices," Joseph said, following the conversation.

"Yes, you are right, and cenotes were Mayan places for sacrifices. They threw in people and jewelry as gifts to the gods. Especially to Chac, the rain god."

"Are we going to swim with skeletons?" Joseph asked, prompting an immediate "Gross!" from Ana.

"Don't worry," Carl said. "This was long time ago, and both treasure hunters and archeologists have been in the cenotes digging out human remains, jewelry, ceramic, and anything else that might have any value. Everything must be gone by now."

"But why did the people die? Didn't they know how to swim?" Ana asked with a worried look on her young face.

"I guess not. Plus, cenotes are actually parts of underground rivers, and some of them, but not the one we are going to, have strong currents that can pull people away from where they went into the water," I said.

"I am scared and I think it will be disgusting to swim there," Ana said.

"If you don't want to swim you don't have to, but people from around here say that this cenote is protected by a little girl." I remembered a story that I had heard long before. It was not exactly this cenote, but the story might work for my daughter.

"How?" she said, waiting. I should have known Ana would not be happy with so little information. The story has a bad part, the loss of a child, and I did not know how she was going to react, but I took a chance.

"Well, there used to be a family that lived around here, and they had a daughter. One day, the daughter went missing and they never found her. Not too long after, neighbors started seeing a small figure around the cenote, and since that time, no young woman or girl has drowned here. The little girl has protected the cenote since then, made it especially safe for a little girl like you," I said and paused. "This does not mean that you can be irresponsible," I finished, just in case, but not worrying too much about Ana, who was always very careful.

"What about Joseph and Daddy?" she asked after thinking for a while.

"We will be fine, we are good swimmers. And maybe we will become messengers of the gods," my husband said with a smile.

"What?" both kids asked with the question written on their faces.

"Mayan legends say that if you come back up after diving into a cenote, the gods are letting you live. And what you say when you come out of the water is a direct message from the gods." But Ana did not follow, and continued to frown. I needed to get serious to convince her.

"Ana, this is a safe place for swimming, specifically allowed by the Mexican government. It's safe to swim, believe me. It is clean, too, a national park where people from around here come to swim all the time."

"Are there any more stories about cenotes?" my son asked. "I want to know about the bad ones with very strong underground currents."

"Yes, there is a story from the time when the Spaniards were trying to conquer Merida. Do you want to hear it?" I asked, happy to change the subject.

"Yes," he said at once.

"The legend says that a Spanish army was attacking a Mayan town that had a small cenote close by. The town's chief decided to hide some women and children for safekeeping inside the caverns surrounding the cenote. When the Spaniards neared the town they encountered strong resistance, but one of their soldiers noticed the people inside the caverns. The Spaniards blocked the cavern exits and demanded that the town's defenders surrender or they would kill all the women and children. When the chief refused, the Spaniards moved toward the caverns to make good on their threat. Suddenly, a lightning bolt crashed into the side of the cenote, making a vault fall down onto the Spaniards."

"Did they all die, even the Mayans?" asked Joseph.

"I think mostly Spaniards, but some Mayans too. The story says that it took another three years for the Spaniards to conquer that village, and by that time, it was only a ghost town. All the citizens had moved."

"That is a sad story even for the Mayan people. They let some of their own people die," Joseph said.

"For the Mayans it was an honor to die for the gods, and this was a direct intervention of the rain god Chac," I said.

"Is this the cenote of that story?"

"No, that was a bigger cenote with a lot of complicated caves. I think this one looks more like a normal pond." I was getting tired of talking with my face turned to the back seat. I ended the conversation and urged the kids to look out the windows to avoid getting sick, but in truth I was the one starting to feel the motion.

We finally arrived at the park. The rest of my family had just arrived in a separate car and were getting out when we pulled in. We had decided in the end to rent a second car to have a little more freedom, which really meant that my American husband would not have to do everything on the timetable of my Mexican family, something that would have driven him insane.

The cenote was small. We could see some small ruins along one side, but by the impressive standards of the region, they were nothing to warrant our attention. The facilities were just two bathrooms and a palm-thatch building where people could change and leave their clothes before getting in the water. Within moments, we were undressed, having put swimming suits under our clothes. Just as we were leaving the building, though, two light-colored, slow-moving bulls walked in front of us, displaying their impressive horns.

"I guess these two gringo bulls are first in line," said a man, making fun of the pale-colored bulls, which are common in this part of Mexico.

The bulls walked past us and started sipping water from the cenote, enjoying a quiet natural break.

"Sorry!" A groundskeeper came running up with his hat in his hands. "The water is used by the farmers around here. They are allowed by the government to do this. You can go to the other side and jump in," the man said, pointing to the other side of the water, just a few yards away.

But as we watched the water and saliva fall from the faces of the bulls into the pool, the thought of swimming became much less attractive.

"I think we are going to pass. We don't want to scare the tourists," my sister said with a smile, pointing to the bulls and my husband and kids. It was obvious they did not want to swim either.

"There is no way I am swimming in the water trough and bath of who knows how many animals," my father said to me, carefully checking that my kids were not listening.

"Oh, well. We have a beautiful beach just twenty minutes away," I said, and a loud sigh of relief came from Ana.

We all rushed out of the ecologic park laughing. Two bullies had just driven us out.

In the car, we all kept quiet. On the way out, I looked back at the cenote and noticed how calm the water looked. The Mayans thought that drowning was caused by the actions of a god. Internal currents would pull people down without warning, and they would disappear into the internal river, never to be seen again.

Once again, I was reminded of my grandmother's life. In all the years we lived together, almost all my life, there was never the hint of a problem. Like the cenote, her calm surface made us think that everything was fine. But everything was not normal, and deep inside she was hiding a secret. Her current did not kill her because over long years she learned how to swim in it. But what had happened to the men in the photo and the two disappearing hands? Were they dead, sucked down by the current? Were they still living as my grandmother did, in a lie?

The city of Progreso, which has the closest beach to Merida, was bigger than I remembered or expected. The name means "progress," which is what people hoped the port would bring to Merida at the beginning of the century. A long, shallow limestone shelf made building the port an engineering challenge. Today, the 2,100-meter long pier is hard to miss, but shows little evidence of the years of toil that went into its making.

The beach was a little crowded, but we managed to find a palapa, or long palm umbrella, where my husband laid out several chairs and our belongings. The sea looked like a turquoise pool, so peaceful and inviting. The beautiful white sand felt like flour under our toes, and even on a day much hotter than this one would not burn our feet. The cool sea breeze blew my hair gently and the rhythmic movement of the small waves made me sleepy.

We had a task to do, though. My sisters and I took leave of the rest of the family, almost against our will, abandoning a picture perfect moment to begin looking for the address of Ramona. An accommodating police officer we saw on our way was kind enough to give us directions to the neighborhood, complicated in a way that can only be found in Mexico.

"We are lost," Ivonne cried, after we drove down the same street for the fifth time. We decided to stop at a convenience store. If it worked the last time, maybe it would work again. We were confident that we were in the right neighborhood.

Five minutes after entering the store, we were in front of Ramona's house. Who needs maps if you have a store on every corner and a small-town culture where everyone knows everyone else?

We did not need to knock on the open door. We peaked inside and saw a group of women sitting on the back patio. They came to greet us. After introductions that involved many hugs from complete strangers, we learned that Ramona was in the back room, the hammock room. We also learned from these women who loved her that Ramona suffered from dementia.

"She is a little crazy," her daughter Maria said. "But her heart is the same, and she will be nice to you. Maybe you can get something from her. She remembers the past better than the present."

Maria walked us to the back room, which held a large wooden machine that took most of the space. Several people were working the machine, which contained an unfinished red hammock in the process of being woven. They stopped when we entered the room.

An old woman was sitting in the corner, a big smile on her face. She looked straight ahead at nothing, and was perfectly still. We crept forward, afraid of startling her. I knelt down to say hello.

She took my hand between her two hands and said with a sweet voice, "Is dinner ready? Did you soak the dough in mint as I told you?" Her big smile contained no teeth, something that made her looked sweeter. Her lips completely disappeared inside her mouth, making her look like she was laughing. It reminded me of the toothless smile of a baby.

"Mom, these people are the family of Aurelio Diaz. They came to visit from Mexico City," Maria said.

"Did you say Diaz? Oh, that is a beautiful family. The house is empty now, a sad story, everyone gone." She looked at us as she said this, but I could tell that she was almost blind.

My sister Mercedes took out my grandmother's photograph and showed it to her, pointing and asking, "Do you know this man with the Diaz girls in the photo?"

She looked at the photo, first very close to her face, then as far away as her arm would allow. Her face looked old, but she did not have many wrinkles. Her eyes were dark brown and vivid. She had long black hair pulled back in a ponytail and it was easy to see that her family was taking good care of her. She looked very clean and did not have the bad smells or dirty clothes sometimes found in people of her age and condition. She wore a beautiful long hipil that covered all her body, even her feet.

"That's Carlos Ancona," she said, pointing at the mystery man. "He is so handsome. --- I need to look good for him. He always comes in the back door and looks at the meals that we are cooking, takes a bite with a spoon, and goes into the front of the house and surprises the poor ladies. Sometimes they are not ready to receive him. If he wasn't so handsome, I would throw him out of the kitchen with a broomstick. --- I need to clean the birdcages. --- Oh, my God! I am going to get in trouble with Jovita!" She ended this standing up and trying to leave the room, but her old body did not cooperate with her mind. She sat down back in her chair, closed her mouth again, and fell asleep within a few minutes.

We left the room embarrassed for intruding, but the warm Maria made us feel comfortable soon.

"We are so sorry to intrude on your family," Ivonne said.

"Don't worry, beautiful. This is the event of the year for us. I am so happy to finally meet someone from the Diaz family. Your relatives were so generous to us. We don't have enough words to thank you."

We knew that our family had given Ramona the house, but we really did not know anything else and it was embarrassing to admit this to Maria. We told her our entire story, sitting on the porch with a couple of the local Montejo beers that we had brought from the convenience store. We hoped that Maria could help us to make some sense of all these memories.

"I was born in the Diaz house. We lived there for years after the family all moved to Mexico City. Your great-grandparents never came back, not even once," Maria said, taking a small sip from her beer.

"Did your mother tell you why?" I asked with a serious tone. I wanted to show her how important this was to us.

"No, not really. She loves your family very much, beautiful," Maria said. She paused, considering. "I think something bad happened, but she never talked about it. She was loyal to the Diaz family and would never say anything bad about them."

"What about you or your sister. Did you see anything?"

"I was born long after the Diaz family was gone. My mother married late in life, and later said that it was because of loneliness. She used to say that for days, she sat alone and the only people who visited her at the Diaz house were the aluxes."

"Aluxes?" I asked.

"Beautiful, how can someone from Merida not know what aluxes are?" Maria said this as a joking recrimination.

"I know they are goblins, but thought they only lived on farms to protect the land and the harvest."

"Ha!" said Maria. "You do not know my mother. She brought them from the farm and civilized them. Thanks to her, they now wear suits and watches." Maria was laughing so hard that we had to join her.

"This is a funny story," she said, pausing and gathering herself for a long speech. "You know how a farmer can go and ask a wizard to make an aluxe to protect his land? There is a big ceremony involved. The wizard makes a clay man, then the farmer introduces the soon-to-be aluxe to all his relatives at a party. The farmer later finds a tree or stone somewhere on the land and hides the clay man. The farmer takes care of the aluxe through the years, leaving presents and food on the spot, especially before harvest time. The aluxe protects the land and spooks undesired visitors."

"I knew part of it," Mercedes said.

"My mother decided that she wanted an aluxe to protect her while she was alone, so she went to a wizard and asked for the clay man. She did not have relatives or friends to introduce him to, so she skipped the party. And thinking that it was strange to place aluxe under a tree without him knowing anyone, she slept with him!" Maria said, raising her voice. "I used to joke with my mother, asking her if I was the daughter of an aluxe!"

By this time, we were all laughing. "That's why I am so short!" she added. I was starting to feel a little guilty about making fun of her mother. Maria calmed down.

"My guess is that she was lonely. My father saved her. He came and rang the doorbell every day to sell fresh bread. They became friends, and I am standing here now."

"That's a sweet story," I said.

"Coming from a baker's family, it is literally sweet, with a lot of licorice flavor," Maria said with a smile.

"And who is that Jovita that your mother mentioned?" I asked, trying to get us back to our purpose.

"She was the woman in charge of the household when my mother was young. I think she moved to the United States. My mother talks about her a lot. When I was young, she kept repeating that she should have gone to school like Jovita wanted. That's why I remember her name," Maria said.

"Do you know anything about Carlos Ancona?"

"No, sorry. I can't recall her ever mentioning him before."

It was close to lunchtime when we ended our conversation. Maria and her family invited us to stay, but I explained that the rest of the family was at the beach waiting for us. She insisted on giving us a large bag full of fried fish, just brought in by the local fishermen that morning. For my kids, she added a pair of chocolate sodas called soldados de chocolate that were typical of Yucatan.

We were in the car ready to leave when Maria came running out of her house with another, more carefully wrapped, package in her hands.

"This is for your family. Please take it," she said in a hurry. "I remember that my mother said that this was made for your grandmother, Señorita Amanda. She never explained to us why she had it, but it is rightfully yours."

We opened the package to see a beautiful hipil, handmade with careful and intricate cross-stitching.

"Those are xtabentum flowers," Maria explained. "They are the wild flowers of Yucatan." With that, she waved goodbye.

We arrived back at the beach that was just minutes away if you knew the route, happy and a little tipsy, except for Ivonne, who was driving. Carl and Joseph were swimming in the sea, while my father, a civil engineer, was making an elaborate sand castle with Ana. We told them the story and showed them the dress. We had interesting new clues, and two more names: Carlos Ancona and Jovita.

We ate the fresh fish on the beach using some paper plates that Maria had put in the bag. My kids loved the fish. It was so fresh that it melted in our mouths despite its crispy exterior.

We drove back to the hotel tired and covered with sand. The hotel room felt clean and fresh when we arrived, and we settled in for the night, happy with our new information.

Chapter 9: The Lost Jacket

Merida, 1924

A young man spent most of a party talking with a beautiful girl. The night was cool, so he gave her his jacket to wear and walked her home. The next day he went back to her house to retrieve his jacket, but when the girl's mother opened the door, he was told that the girl had been dead for six months. After his denials and assurances that he had seen her the night before, the girl's mother took him to the cemetery, where, to the surprise of everyone, they found his jacket on top of the girl's grave.

- Cuban Story

The mind can be the last part of the body to realize that it is free.

Amanda was preparing to leave Merida, but the process took longer than expected. Her father had agreed to her departure, but she needed to find the right school. She chose Bryn Mawr College outside Philadelphia, founded by Quakers but by now a non-denominational school. She picked Bryn Mawr not only because of its academic reputation, but also because for many years the school had had a woman president, Carey Thomas.

As a young woman, Thomas had gone to Europe to pursue her dream of earning a graduate degree. American schools denied her (and all women) that privilege, so she took her dreams to another country, just as Amanda was now doing. Thomas had helped establish Bryn Mawr to remedy this situation, and Amanda considered it an honor to be accepted. She was going to work hard.

Alma Reed wrote during this time. She was in New Orleans, but ready to return to Merida. She was waiting for De La Huerta to be defeated, which was looking more and more likely. He had never made it to Mexico City, and Plutarco Elias Calles, the newly elected president, looked strong. The revolt was weakening over time.

An apology for the death of Carillo Puerto came to the people of Yucatan from the central government in Mexico City. The newspapers were already calling him a martyr, a Mexican Abraham Lincoln.

Amanda's relationship with her mother was better, and every day she woke up early and opened her door at the moment her mother was dropping her breakfast. She would attempt small talk, but her mother always fled. On the day of her last breakfast at home, she managed to give her mother a hug. It was their first long hug in Amanda's memory. Her mother smelled like baby powder.

Finally, in early May, after a three-month process of selection, application and acceptance, Amanda was on her way. She was bringing all of Cacho's papers and school records with her, too. Despite her lack of equal opportunity, Cacho was a great student, even better than Amanda was. Amanda hoped that she could convince the college to accept Cacho as well. She carried recommendation letters from her father and the high school principal.

Amanda's father drove her to Progreso with trembling hands and hundreds of warnings about what to do or not to do. It was Amanda's first trip without a chaperone, and he worried about her reputation. Amanda was too excited to care.

She was taking the ship Yucatan to Manhattan. She hoped that the boring name was not an omen for her trip. The ship was crowded with young men going to study abroad or visiting New York for business. Her father told her to stay away from them.

Amanda's father had made the trip to New York on numerous occasions, but business was keeping him home this time. He had arranged for someone to pick her up at Manhattan and take her to the school.

They arrived at the dock hours before departure and moved her bags onto a small boat that would take them to the Yucatan, which was anchored three miles from shore. Her father followed Amanda onto the small boat, and she felt very happy for his company. She was going to miss him a great deal. The small boat started to move into the clear water, with the sun strong above them. Amanda looked down into the water and had no difficulty seeing all the way to the bottom.

After few minutes of rowing into deeper water, they discovered new companions, four sharks that had surrounded the boat. The stealthy creatures weaved around the boat, making almost no noise or ripple in the water.

"I wish I had brought a knife or a net. My family would be having a good dinner tonight," joked one of the rowers, as drops of sweat fell from his face.

Amanda was not laughing. She had never liked the sharks found in the area of Progreso, and today they looked particularly threatening, as if put there to remind her of the perils of the journey she was beginning. For the first time, she felt afraid. She was leaving her secure and loving family and venturing into a world where no one would be there to protect her. She scooted next to her father and hugged him, the kind of unrestrained hug that a child gives and that she had not done in many years. In that moment, she felt how hard it was to break apart and fly away in pursuit of her dream, which might be an impossible dream.

The four sharks disappeared as suddenly as they had appeared. They were making way for two approaching whale sharks. The whale sharks were as big as the boat, but the gentle giants seemed to take little notice of them. Their spotted backs flew by fast, going north. They were so close to the boat that Amanda was able to put her hand out and touch the back of one of them, feeling a flow of energy run through her body. She would need that energy later.

Once they boarded the Yucatan, Amanda's father talked with every single person they encountered. He introduced himself to a recently married couple who were traveling to Manhattan on their honeymoon and asked them to take care of Amanda. Cristina and Fernando Gallo had the stateroom next to Amanda's, and they became her companions throughout the journey.

Amanda's father finished his visit and said his goodbyes, finishing by giving the ship's captain a fine Serrano ham from Spain for the trip. The captain clapped him on the back several times and promised to take care of his precious daughter.

Amanda hurried to unpack in her stateroom and rushed to the deck for a final view of the beautiful beaches and palms of Yucatan, something she would remember later like a postcard. The beach grew smaller, and soon there was nothing but water surrounding Amanda.

The ship felt much larger that Amanda expected. What an incredible machine this was. The power of these engines would sail her far away in a slow, continuous way. The two funnels with steam coming from them left paths of small, graceful clouds, which became part of the new sky, the new adventure.

The wide path around the ship had room for both deck chairs and a promenade. Through windows near her, Amanda could see the main dining room, which took up a large portion of the center of this deck. The dining room was crowded with elaborate chairs and tables covered in crisp white linens. Amanda wondered idly whether all that furniture was nailed to the floor.

The somber white that covered all visible walls contrasted with the fun, colorful dress of people on the deck. The spotless floor reflected the sun, and from a distance it looked as if people were walking on a bed of starlight.

Amanda found a deck chair, sat down to read a book, and let the hours fly by. The number of strangers who passed her by made Amanda realize just how alone she was.

After one day at sea, they arrived at Cuba, the Pearl of the Antilles. The ship had organized a tour, and Amanda decided to join.

Havana had narrow streets and romantic colonial balconies. The small tour group walked the promenades and the famous Prado Boulevard with sun umbrellas for the women and broad straw hats for the men.

Looking across her tour group that morning, Amanda first saw those eyes, two light blue eyes that reminded her of father's eyes and Carlos' eyes. Those eyes would follow Amanda throughout this trip, follow her everywhere, even in her sleep. Amanda's life was surrounded by blue eyes, something rare for Mexico.

They drank rum and sparkling water flavored with mint and lime, called mojitos, at the Sloppy Joe's bar and toured a large cigar factory. While some of the group went to a casino, Amanda and ten other people, including the blue eyes, visited a voodoo ritual.

In a small house near the Guanabacoa beach, listening to rumba music and again sipping mojitos, they submitted to a voodoo spell of purification. Rhythmic bongo drums made Amanda's body vibrate, while her gaze continued to return to the blue eyes. The rattle of the maracas added to the explosion of noise, making the sound of fast falling water hitting hard soil and breaking into bouncing drops. Amanda closed her eyes and felt elevated above everyone else in the room. Near the end of the ceremony, she felt the soft pressure of someone's hand on her back and a warm breeze in her ear, and her body curled with pleasure. When the music stopped, Amanda opened her eyes to see herself surrounded by the same dull people. The blue eyes were gone.

Back on the ship, she realized that she was enchanted with this new country and all that she had learned of its politics. The president, Alberto Zayas, reminded her of Felipe Carrillo Puerto, a strong idealistic socialist, but no Communist. Like Felipe Carrillo Puerto, he had given women the right to vote. The entire city of Havana reflected his government. It showed every sign of being vibrant and prosperous.

Alas, before he was elected president, Zayas had opposed the treaty that gave the United States the rights to

Guantanamo, and now the United States opposed his government. Elections would be held a year from now and there were rumors that he was not seeking reelection. It was a pity.

The trip to Nassau was smooth despite warnings that crossing the West Indies could be a challenge due to shallow waters and coral reefs that mysteriously emerged from the water or vanished overnight. The sea was beautiful, and several times schools of dolphins swam alongside the boat, bringing everyone onto the deck.

It was during one of these dolphin episodes that Amanda met the man with the blue eyes. His name was Alberto Molina and he was an acquaintance of the Gallos. The four of them agreed to have dinner together that evening.

Amanda chose her best dress for the occasion. She arrived in the main dining room a little late, not wanting to risk being alone at their table. Fortunately, the Gallos and Alberto were already there, having what appeared to be a lively conversation.

The table seated six, and Amanda was having a hard time deciding where to sit when the waiter interrupted, announcing that the other couple assigned to their table was feeling sick and that Amanda's group would be moved to a table for four. They sat at corner table, the light a bit dim for reading the menu, but great for conversation.

As Alberto held her chair for her to sit, Amanda felt a jolt of electricity. She was very nervous.

Alberto spoke first. "I can't believe that we have never met! I have spoken to your father several times at his store, and he has even invited me to parties at his house. A pity, but my work always interfered at the last moment."

"My father must have liked you to extend the invitations," said Amanda. "He is always cautious about whom he invites, unlike my sister Julieta, who invites everyone in the city."

"Well, I never met her before either," said Alberto. "I did hear about the parties at your house from Carlos Ancona, though, and..."

"You know Carlos?" interrupted Amanda.

"Yes, he and I worked together for a time. He mentioned that he went to your house often, and really enjoyed it. You and he... are not dating, are you?" asked Alberto.

"No," answered Amanda, a little embarrassed that everyone assumed the she was having a relationship with Carlos.

"What type of work were you doing with Carlos?" asked Fernando Gallo, finally causing Alberto to look away from Amanda and giving her a chance to regard him more carefully.

Alberto was a tall man who had light brown, short, curly hair, a fair complexion, and something in the way he talked that broadcast self-confidence. He had dimples and a perpetual half smile on his face. And, of course, those blue eyes. Amanda felt a strong attraction to him, which surprised her, as she had never felt something like this so fast before.

"I am a civil engineer and was working on the construction of the highway to Chichen-Itza while Carlos was writing the tourist books for the ruins. In fact, this trip is related to my work. I am researching America's Lincoln Highway, and my intention is to drive it coast-to-coast. The highway was built with money diverted from the marble for the Lincoln Memorial. Americans are so practical! Even more interesting for a civil engineer, some parts of this highway are paved in concrete, a fashion I hope Mexico will follow soon." After answering, Alberto looked back at Amanda in a way that made her wonder if he was feeling the same attraction.

"This will take you a long time, won't it Alberto?" asked Fernando.

"I will be traveling for a year. I want to take my time and visit the important cities on my way. Maybe try to have a few meetings with the highway's builders and..."

"What does your fiancée think about all this?" Cristy Gallo interrupted, sensing the connection developing between Amanda and Alberto and wanting to warn her. This came as a shock to Amanda, and she held her breath waiting for the reply.

Alberto looked at Cristy as she spoke, but turned to Amanda as he answered. "Nothing, really. We..."

"Come on, Cristy," Fernando said, not allowing Albert to finish. "That question is much too personal."

"No problem," Alberto said, but changed the subject by asking Amanda: "Why are you traveling to New York?"

"I am going to school," Amanda said proudly. "I was accepted at the Bryn Mawr College outside Philadelphia."

"Wow!" Alberto exclaimed. "You are different! That's a prestigious school." He smiled and turned to Fernando, nodding with something that looked like admiration.

"What do you plan to study?" Fernando asked.

"I think chemistry. But I have time to change my mind later. This summer will be about getting oriented, and then I will start by taking basic courses. I definitely do not want to major in English," Amanda said.

"Because you want to return to Mexico," Alberto said in a voice almost like a whisper as he read her mind.

"Yes," Amanda said, and for some reason her eyes filled with tears. She turned her attention to her soup, which was getting cold. She worried that everyone could read her emotions.

The conversation moved to safer topics, the food and the various passengers. Alberto had plenty of funny comments about the situations on the ship, and kept everyone laughing. The night flew by and before they knew it, they were leaving the table and losing the chance to get to know each other better.

It took two beautiful days of sailing to reach Nassau. The days were warm, clear, and peaceful, but the nights were even better. Amanda woke up in the middle of each night, went out on the deck, and watched the stars. On her second night out, she noticed a shadow behind her. She knew who it was. It was easy to identify his tall figure. She turned around and looked straight at him, but the night was dark and they could not see each other's faces clearly. She felt his eyes searching her face and body. They faced each other for a long time, sharing the breeze and smells of the ocean, without saying a word. Amanda's heart beat faster, in harmony with the waves hitting the hull of the ship, the sound of the ocean its own form of pleasure. The desire and humidity of Amanda's body almost made her lose her balance. They parted at sunrise, as the first rays of sunlight exploded over the horizon.

Back in her room, Amanda felt guilty for all these sensations. She thought about Carlos, but his eyes were disappearing from her mind. She fell asleep and dreamed that Alberto's hands were touching her.

Nassau, nine hundred miles from Manhattan, was another small paradise, but there was no opportunity for the passengers to disembark. Amanda imagined the old buccaneers' island as a real haven. The strategic position, beautiful beaches, and liberal government made Nassau exotic and adventurous. The real freedoms offered by the island made fun of her small temporary freedom. Amanda may have been on a quest to change her destiny, but at least for now, she was inside a new jail, the ship she was using as transportation.

She was standing at the deck rail as the ship left Nassau when Alberto appeared at her side.

"Do you know what Blackbeard the pirate used to say?" he asked, looking at the diminishing island.

"No," Amanda said quietly, trying to control the trembling in her hands as they sat lightly on the rail.

"Make your own hell, and see how long you can bear it." Alberto said this looking at her, but turned and disappeared as suddenly as he had arrived.

Alberto's words were puzzling to Amanda. Was he living in the same hell that she was? Her desire for him was so strong that she could start a hellfire, creating a hell for both of them that would break many hearts.

Amanda stayed on deck for a long time, past sundown, and let the darkness surround her. Later, in complete darkness, some noise came from the stern of the ship on the port side.

Amanda strolled toward that area of the ship. Staying back in the shadows, she saw a group of men on-boarding boxes from a small boat flying the flag of the Bahamas. The tinkle of glass bottles hitting each other seemed a perfect accompaniment to the twinkling reflection of the dim moon on the water. The operation ended within minutes, and a dozen boxes disappeared into the ship. The small boat disappeared, and the show was over. Amanda returned to her stateroom, where weariness soon overcame her.

The rest of the trip went by without incident. The water changed from light blue to dark, and a light rain drove most passengers to stay indoors. She did not see Alberto again and no longer went outside in the middle of the night. She was afraid of her feelings for him. By the time the ship arrived in New York after five and a half days of traveling, Amanda longed for his company.

Entering the United States through New York was fantastic. The skyline of buildings was impressive, and the size of the city unimaginable to someone from Merida. Amanda said hello to the Statue of Liberty, but the somber lady did not respond.

Amanda was equal parts excited and anxious. Speaking English full-time would be a challenge, and one that she would begin to face right away. Someone from the school was to meet her at the entry port, and Amanda was already silently rehearsing her own introduction.

She had been to the U.S. consulate in Merida and had all her immigration papers in order. But she had always been a bit afraid of authority and did not want to end up like the people she had read about being detained at Ellis Island. But most of those were Europeans entering without proper paperwork, and the Yucatan's captain explained to Amanda that even without papers the immigration authorities would not reject first- and second-class passengers. The U.S. liked rich people.

The captain was right, everything went smoothly, and she breezed through immigration. Before she knew it, she was outside looking for a sign from the school or some other indication of someone waiting for her. All the passengers she recognized from the Yucatan were gone and Amanda was beginning to feel alarmed when she saw Alberto walking toward her with a broad smile.

"What are you doing here?" he asked while taking a cigarette from his pocket and lighting it up.

"No one came for me," she said, thinking how lucky she was to see someone she knew.

"This is the thing," he said. "I can stand here and pretend I know nothing about your circumstances and waste our time. Or... " he placed a finger over Amanda's lips to keep her from speaking, "...I can just tell you that I sent away your welcoming party with a little white lie about you missing the boat." He said this with another smile and a look of mischief in his blue eyes. He smelled like tobacco and salt.

She laughed and he laughed with her. After a few minutes of that, they embraced, holding their arms around each other's waists. He caressed her hair.

"My guess is that the school will try to contact your family. You need to send them a telegram right away saying that you couldn't find the person who was to meet you, but that the captain of the ship helped you and you are on your way, safe and sound. You should notify the school that there has been a mix-up, too. And the two of us, we can have a wonderful day together, at last." He tossed away his cigarette.

"That sounds great, but after our wonderful day how will I get to my school?" Amanda asked, gazing into his eyes. They were now holding hands, and she could feel his strong grip.

He looked back at her almost without blinking, and she thought she saw a slight trembling around his mouth.

"You are going to have a personal driver, me, after a great lunch in Manhattan," Alberto said, finally kissing her.

They looked at each other and knew. There was nothing else to say.

He drove her to the school six hours later, and then he was gone. All that remained was the smell of him on her body, something to prove he existed, like the lost jacket in the story. He was now a phantom, but every minute Amanda had spent with him was as valuable to her as years. She might be emotionally confused, but she began this new chapter with a new appreciation of life.

Would she see Alberto again? He had felt so real, so full of passion. They both had said words of love, but was he feeling them as Amanda was? He was engaged, and Amanda had not touched on that topic at all during the past six hours. But he had promised to stay in contact, and Amanda hoped that her judgment of his character was right and he would come back into her life when they both were ready for something else.

Chapter 10: Henequen

Chicago, 1924

A wise man called Zamná was walking through an open field of henequen when one of the long spines cut through his hand and injured him badly. One of his students cut off the plant spine and pounded it against a stone as punishment. As the plant disintegrated, it revealed a set of strong fibers, and Zamná said, "Life and pain come together."

- Mayan Legend

Chicago was beautiful. It was the last week of September, but the sky was blue and the temperature felt just right. Amanda was staying at the Drake Hotel in a room overlooking Lake Michigan. The wonderful blue lake reminded her of the Gulf of Mexico off Yucatan, but the colors here were more vivid. The combination of the lake's blue with the green grass and the pale sand was intense. It was strange for Amanda to see a beach without palm trees and to think that for part of each year the water was frozen and the beach covered in snow.

Amanda had travelled to Chicago to meet Cacho. When she had arrived at her school in May, she wrote a letter to Alma Reed asking for help in finding Cacho, hoping that Cacho had also reached out to Alma when she had escaped months ago. Cacho had.

Alma was helping Cacho with some money, but she really did not know anything else about her. Amanda wrote to Cacho at the address that Alma gave her, and set up a time to visit. The letters between them looked more like office memos than the correspondence between long-time friends. They would reunite tomorrow.

Leading up to this, Amanda learned how deeply Alma was grieving for Felipe Carrillo Puerto. She hoped that Alma could join her in Chicago, but Alma could not find the strength for the trip. It was nice enough that she was helping Cacho financially, Amanda knew.

The general who had killed Felipe Carrillo Puerto set himself up as governor and remained in power in Merida for some time, enjoying parties with the *Casta Divina*, who had never appreciated Carrillo Puerto's socialist ideas. His leader, De La Huerta, was still in Veracruz, but it seemed just matter of time before the federal army would capture him. Meanwhile, the enemy occupied Merida.

The federal government in Mexico City forbade the sale or transportation of henequen as a way of punishing both the unlawful governor in Merida and the hacienda owners who supported him. Even so, Amanda thought that the sanctions were too moderate.

The United States started with a policy of not dealing with any supporters of De La Huerta, but the situation was changing. As the world started running out of the precious henequen and sisal fiber, the lack of the product began to put stress on the relationship between the United States and Mexico. The U.S. announced that more delays in delivery could cause "long distance effects."

Those were scary days for Amanda, who read the news from a small room at her school in a foreign country that was sounding more aggressive. She cringed at the thought that the rebels and hacienda owners would be enriched by henequen money, but an invasion by the United States would be far worse. There was a rumor that U.S. Marines were busy training to go to the Yucatan peninsula.

The Mexican government finally allowed the sale of henequen, but did not give any support in transportation. U.S. ships were allowed to get the "green gold" themselves from Progreso, and the situation calmed down. Capitalism was winning out, and the injustice of it was that the assassins of Felipe Puerto were large beneficiaries.

Fortunately, after a few months the general who had killed Felipe Carrillo Puerto was out of Merida. He fled the city without offering resistance when the federal army finally marched into town. He had enriched himself to the point where he could live a full, rich life in any county of the world, and no longer felt the need to fight. As far as Yucatan was concerned, the De La Huerta coup was over.

The end of the rebellion gave Alma the opportunity to return to Merida. Felipe's ex-wife had returned to Merida from Cuba, where she had lived for years, to assume the role of widow of the martyr. As only the last girlfriend of Felipe Carrillo Puerto, Alma received no attention this time, and was fine with it. She just wanted to see Felipe's city once again. For the rest of her life, Merida would be close to her heart. The white bohemian city filled with the smell of vanilla said goodbye to their love with rain unusual for the season.

Amanda had a whole day in Chicago before her meeting with Cacho. She was going to use it to explore the city.

Coming out of the Drake, she was astonished to see that the area just east of the hotel contained industrial factories and low-rent residences. It was very peculiar to see the magnificent hotel next to poor housing. The neighborhood was just starting to change. Amanda mused that this would be a good place to invest in land.

The scenery changed rapidly. Standing in the old Pine Street, now an extension of Michigan Avenue, Amanda saw beautiful houses and a wide street where fancy cars were filled with passengers enjoying the lovely day.

Amanda decided to walk to the beach. The day was pleasant and she wanted to touch the water. The size of the lake was impressive, and it was hard to believe that it was unsalted water. It must be very hard to swim, she thought.

The beach was crowded, with many more men than women bathing. Most people were getting wet only to their knees and not really swimming. Everyone wore suits in the same style: all black, with shorts and a vest with a round neck. Gentlemen had exchanged their typical tall hats for flat straw hats adorned with black ribbons.

Eager to touch the water, Amanda took off her shoes and approached the shoreline, only to have a small wave surge up and wet her entire skirt. The water was surprisingly cold, certainly by the standards of the tropical Gulf of Mexico. Amanda could not believe that people were in that cold water. She would drink water this temperature on a warm day in Merida and think that it was too cold!

Walking back on Michigan Avenue, shivering with a wet skirt and with shoes full of sand, she decided that after changing, she would go shopping and visit the famous department stores of Marshall Field and Carson Pirie Scott on State Street. Amanda would be able to buy new shoes and clothes, and maybe a coat for the coming winter. There were certainly no winter coats to be found in Merida.

The walk from the hotel was long, and on the way, she would need to cross the first double-decker drawbridge in the world. By the time she arrived at the Chicago River, the bridge was going up to allow through a stream of sailboats returning to the city. The bridge's mechanism impressed her with its size and precision. Watching the boats line up and pass through was like something at a carnival. All she needed were music and a glass of beer.

After a while, the wait became wearying. Car traffic around the open bridge was terrible, and Amanda saw her first traffic jam. The sounds of the different motors and the smell of the exhaust began to make her a little sick. And there were people everywhere.

Amanda must have shown some of her distress, for a woman standing next to her said with a smile, "This is the blood of our industry, lady. Calm down."

She felt silly, standing in one of the busiest and most interesting cities in the world, complaining. "I need new shoes," Amanda said, giving the woman an apologetic look.

"Well, you are going the right way."

"Thanks," Amada said. "So if the river is the blood, what is the heart?" she added, joking.

"Oh, Chicago has a rusty iron heart, just like mine," she laughed.

"Excuse me?" Amanda did not grasp her meaning.

"The elevated train, the El," she said. But the bridge was going down and people were moving, so the woman sped away from Amanda, saying goodbye with a short wave of her hand as if she had something very important to do.

Amanda crossed the river and saw that it looked green but not very deep. There were many boats moving away from them and Amanda turned to admire a scene that seemed to her to be out of a futuristic story, with tall buildings fronting the busy river.

As she looked north from the south side of the river, she admired a white building that she later learned was the Wrigley Building, from the Wrigley chewing gum empire. When she learned this, she thought back on the irony of standing in front of a Chicago building so beautiful that had been financed through the natural resources of Yucatan.

Gum was big in both Yucatan and Quintana Roo, the neighboring state. For generations, the Mayans had been collecting the sap from the sapodilla tree, mixing it with a few other ingredients, and forming it into squares of naturally sweet chicle for chewing. "Chiclets" had even made its way into modern English as a name for chewing gum.

Chicle was sold everywhere in Merida, and Amanda remembered how Jovita would shout at her and Cacho every time that she saw them chewing.

"You are going to ruin your teeth! And, it is not proper for a young lady," she would say. It is hard to escape from what you are, Amanda realized. Any little thing can remind you of home.

Amanda arrived at the Marshall Field store hungry and thirsty. She walked through the main doors and almost lost her breath when she saw the quantity and variety of beautiful merchandise. After a snack at the coffee shop, she set herself to the pleasant task of buying new shoes, a couple of dresses, and, of course, the coat.

It took her the rest of the day and visits to several stores, and when she came out of the last store, it was getting dark. With arms full of large bags, a long way to her hotel, and no knowledge of local transportation, Amanda became a bit alarmed. Her family did not know where she was (in fact, thought she was at her college, and never would have approved of her taking this trip on her own). And her roommate had tried to scare her about Chicago, showing her a magazine story describing how two young men had kidnapped and killed a boy just for "experimenting and sensation."

"Chicago is a dangerous place," her roommate said. "And don't forget about Al Capone."

Amanda did not know much about Al Capone, but at this moment, she could not forget him. She feared that he was there watching her from a parked car, or perhaps preparing for a gang fight that would soon cause her to find herself engulfed by gunshots.

"This is crazy," Amanda thought. She had grown up during the violent Mexican Revolution and just lived through the rebellion that claimed Felipe Carrillo Puerto, and she never felt this scared. She looked around, and everyone looked friendly enough, if a bit busy.

Still, the walk back to the hotel seemed too great a challenge in the approaching darkness. Amanda had also thought to visit other places, like the Art Institute of Chicago, but standing on the "busiest corner in the world" overwhelmed her.

Amanda walked back into the store, stood to the side, and tried to calm down. She was on the verge of having a panic attack. She thought about calling a car, but for some reason at that moment could not seem to remember English.

The words came into her head, but she could not find the way to speak them.

After what seemed a long time, she saw a friendly looking figure, a woman cleaning empty shelves in the corner. She was short and dark-skinned, and had a smile on her face. Amanda felt so relieved that she rushed over next to her. She waited for the woman to finish her job, perhaps standing a little too close to her.

The woman saw her, looked down, and was about to walk away when Amanda shouted in Spanish, “Wait, I need help!”

The woman’s expression brightened, and the smile came back to her face. “You speak Spanish?” she said in the same language.

“Of course I do. I am Mexican,” Amanda said, now returning the smile.

“You scared me. I was supposed to start cleaning after the store closed, but today I want to go home a little early so I started cleaning early. My manager does not want me working while the customers are still here. He said it is a bad image for the store.” She looked around, checking for her manager.

“He should not treat you like that. You could be a customer yourself,” Amanda said.

“Oh, no, this store is not for Mexicans like me. This store is for rich people. Don’t worry, it’s fine. I have a great job, get paid more than most of my friends, and it is just cleaning. Are you all right? Did you say that you needed help?” she said in a concerned voice.

“Yes. I need a ride to my hotel, but I don’t know how or where to call for one. Do you happen to know what can I do?”

"For you, it's easy. The store will call you a car. You can ask the person who helped you when you were buying your things," she said, pointing at Amanda's packages.

It all worked as she had said, and Amanda was soon back at the Drake. Once in her room, Amanda's thoughts returned to the woman at the store. This was not the first time that she had been uncomfortable about the treatment of Mexicans. She had noticed it before at school, and even here at the hotel. Discrimination was a hard word to use, but to be sure, she received unusual treatment. Americans acted surprised to learn that she was Mexican. They looked at each other in a way that made Amanda feel as if they were deciding in a secret language whether she was going to be accepted.

She had heard from friends in Merida that some hotels in the United States would not accept Mexicans or blacks as guests, though many were employees. This made her become extra nice to the staff, and be a little excessive when it came to gratuities.

On the train to Chicago, Amanda had sat next to a wealthy couple who were traveling to the city on holiday. They had acted very surprised to hear that she was Mexican, and more surprised to learn that she was studying at a prestigious women's college. They called some friends over to share the news, and between laughs, they made Amanda feel like a carnival novelty act. They could not believe that Bryn Mawr College had accepted a woman from Mexico or that Amanda's preparatory education was at a level with that in the United States.

"Does your family have sisal farms? Did you have an American governess who prepared you?" They asked all these things without reservation, as if they were certain that everyone in Mexico was uneducated and that Amanda would be boastful about having an American tutor.

"No, I just went to school with all my friends," Amanda said. "I learned my English at regular school and through a friendly woman who had retired with her husband in Merida. My academic education is 100 % Mexican, at least until the past few months."

It seemed that these Americans had no idea of what Mexico really was, or that Merida, while small, was one of the wealthiest cities in the world. She challenged them to visit Mexico City and see some of the most beautiful architecture on the continent, some of it dating back four hundred years.

"We have one of the largest downtown squares in the world, beautiful old cathedrals and palaces, and church altars covered in gold."

At one of the stops, Amanda changed seats on the train. She was getting too worked up, and she felt surprised and a little embarrassed over her strong feelings. It was a new feeling for her to be the one who was different.

It was true that Mexico was a country with plenty of troubles, but it was eye-opening for Amanda to see it from far away. The years of the Revolution and the uncertainty that followed it had brought many Mexican immigrants to United Sates for the first time. The majority of them were just normal people escaping the poverty and the insecurity of the moment. They had nothing left in Mexico, and nothing to lose by crossing the border. These people did not know English and were taking the lowest, hardest jobs in the market.

A few of the immigrants had been members of Porfirio Diaz's government before the Revolution. These educated people with perfect English blended easily into American society, but they were the exception. In general, Americans treated Mexicans as an inferior race.

On the train, Amanda felt furious and sad. She felt humiliation for the first time in her life. The situation she faced here in the United States was the opposite of the one she had always enjoyed as a member of Merida's upper class. She was now a second-class citizen, and she did not like it.

Defensiveness and patriotism played a role in her feelings, too. It felt like people were criticizing Mexico and home, making critical statements without knowing the whole truth, or making judgments from a single photograph or from hearsay. Amanda herself felt judged through this, and wanted to shout out that there was more to her than her nationality.

That couple on the train thought that they were being nice when they made comments like, "You must be so happy to be here," or "What a privilege you have to be here in the United States." Yes, the country was beautiful and most of the people were nice, but saying that diminished Amanda's country, which was also beautiful. It was a privilege to be Mexican. And it was naïve of these people to think that the United States did not face the same kinds of problems with poverty and class inequality. It was as if they lived in a glass castle or an imaginary world.

Amanda knew that she was overreacting. She was being a little too fast to take offense, and the language barrier was not helping matters. Mexicans, poor or rich, came to the United Sates looking for something that was lacking in Mexico. Pay for regular workers, access to higher education, and women's rights were all better here. In the United States, it was possible for a woman to pursue serious studies at the university level, something that Amanda had seen was far from the case in Mexico.

It was ironic that a similar situation had faced the former head of Bryn Mawr, Carey Thomas, who was forced to go to Europe to study because graduate programs in the United States were not open to women. Perhaps Amanda would become a Latin American pioneer, and many other young women from Mexico would soon follow her path. The decade-long Revolution had halted the wheels of progress bringing Mexico into the modern world, but it was time for all that to change.

Despite her determination to further her education, it had been difficult for Amanda to leave Mexico. She left behind everything, her family, her friends, and her culture. She deeply missed the little things that happened in her daily life.

She missed the baker she had known since she was a young girl who gave her a piece of special bread each morning. She missed the warmth of her schoolmates, who always welcomed her with a smile, a kiss, and a hug, and never forgot to ask, "How are you?" She missed the daily dinner with her father, sharing both a three-course meal and the local and international news.

And she missed the smell of her land and the way a single word could bring on sensations, picture, sounds, and memories of her life. This did not happen to her now that she spoke English all the time, in the way that a joke is only funny if it is understood immediately.

She was on her own here, living alone for the first time in her life, and it was hard to adapt. She had become friends with a few girls at school, but they were new friends, and strong friendship comes with time and shared moments.

Learning a new culture did not help, either, and as she started at college, Amanda ran into situations that were strange for her. She could be standing in the hallway in a conversation with two classmates when one of them would invite the other somewhere, ignoring Amanda, as if she were not there or she were deaf. Amanda would pretend not to hear, and would go on with whatever she was doing, but she could not imagine a situation like that happening in polite society in Mexico. Maybe the language was a barrier or Amanda's accent made the other girls think that she would not understand their conversation.

It was not that everyone in her circle in Mexico was friends with everyone else. But people seemed to pay more attention to social graces and avoiding giving offense to anyone. There was a group of popular girls whom a younger Amanda saw as the picture of the snobby, selfish princesses that she had despised her whole life. Amanda and Cacho had been at war with that group since they where kids, starting with practical jokes played on Gracielita, the group's leader. Still, they were always polite to each other in public.

There was an old saying in Mexico: "Being polite does not make you a coward." While it sometimes took a great deal of effort to say hello to Gracielita and her group, it always helped keep things under control. They had their differences and would never be friends, but they were all human and maintained a certain degree of respect.

Those ground rules did not seem to apply here in the U.S. Many girls at Bryn Mawr ignored Amanda. She was always polite to them and said pleasant hellos, but they positioned themselves in a way that made it clear that she was not welcome, and it would be impossible for her to join the conversations.

Eventually, Amanda decided to seek out others who shared her challenges, and became friends with many of the other foreign students. This group became strong. Not only did their individual loneliness make them more eager to form strong friendships, but also, they had the support of many teachers, who were pleased with the different cultures represented and the strong work ethic that was common to these young women. In just the four months she had been there before her trip to Chicago, Amanda's situation at Bryn Mawr was much improved.

***

That night at the Drake Hotel, Amanda fell asleep with all these thoughts in her mind. Sure, she had some problems, but they were the simple problems of someone her age. She felt young and happy again, like the teenager she actually was. She wanted to enjoy life, and, if possible, share it with Cacho.

Amanda woke up the next morning after a fitful night of sleep. She was so excited to see Cacho again that she was not sure she could bear it. She was supposed to meet her in the lobby at 11:00 a.m., but went down with an hour to spare, found a chair, and sat down to wait. She had brought a book, but found she could not read it. At 10:45, she walked out of the building, hoping to catch Cacho as she walked in. Then she worried that Cacho would enter the hotel from another door, and would miss her. Finally, she worried that the Drake's lobby did not have many windows and that this dim setting was not the ideal meeting place for two best friends reuniting after a long separation.

Hours went by and Cacho did not come. Amanda just sat there waiting, looking so pale that several people asked her if she were all right. She could not believe that Cacho was not there. Three hours went by, but still, she did not move. As Amanda's despair worsened, a blond woman in a long gray coat ran into the hotel lobby speaking in a loud voice. Amanda could not understand her at first, but then realized she was calling her name.

"I'm Amanda," she said, rushing to meet the woman.

"Oh, my God! Sorry I am so late, but I couldn't find anyone to drive me until my brother came home from his job," she said, so rapidly she was almost skipping words. "My name is Marta, and I am a good friend of Carmen's. I am so glad to meet you."

"But where is Cacho, I mean, Carmen?" Amanda asked.

"Don't worry too much. She is sick, and I wouldn't let her leave her bed," Marta said.

"Sick? What? Is she all right?" Amanda asked with a worried look on her face.

"More or less. She is a very stubborn woman, and hid her condition for a long time. But I could hear her coughing down the hallway in my room, especially at night. I even asked her if she was coughing blood. She always said no until this morning, when she fainted in her room and I saw the dirty handkerchiefs."

"Oh, my God. But..."

"Let's talk in the car. My brother is waiting in front of the hotel and needs to get back to work, so please come along," Marta said, rushing Amanda toward the door.

Outside, Marta's brother was parked nearby. He had an old Ford Model T, which looked as if it could break down at any moment.

"Don't worry," said the man at the wheel, whose name turned out to be Pavel. "Carmen says that this car is like a Mexican donkey. It may be stubborn, but will keep running if I am a good owner and take good care of it. Looks aren't everything."

Amanda got into the car with Marta next to her. The three of them began the bumpy ride. The noise of the engine was so loud that it was almost impossible to talk. The worried face of Marta gave Amanda some reassurance. Cacho had found a good friend here, and one who was caring for her. Amanda was anxious about Cacho's condition. She knew that Cacho was strong, and had never even seen her sick. Amanda would take care of her from now on, and she would get better soon.

Pavel talked without pause. But with all the noise, Amanda could only hear pieces of what he was saying. Marta whispered an apology, "He talks when he is nervous." Even that was hard to hear.

They drove through the city streets slowly but steadily, listening to Pavel's stories. He said that this kind of car handled hills better in reverse, for some reason that Amanda did not understand. He talked about the types of wheels, and that the car was running on ethanol. This fuel was inexpensive for them because a farmer friend gave it to them at a great discount.

When the traffic eased, Marta and Amanda could attempt a conversation.

"Carmen is a wonderful girl," Marta said.

"I know. I miss her so much," Amanda said.

"She has been our Angel. I met her through another Mexican woman when we were working on the meat packing line."

"Did Cacho, I mean, Carmen work with you?" Amanda asked, trying to sound normal, feeling a squeeze on her heart over the hard manual labor and the waste of Cacho's abilities, but not wanting to hurt Marta's feelings.

"Yes. She did for a while and she was good, very fast. Then she met Mary McDowell. We all knew who she was, 'the Angel of the Stockyards.' Few of us had ever spoken more than a few words to her, but not Carmen. When she learned who this was, she went right up, introduced herself in perfect English, and offered to volunteer with some of Mary's programs.

"Carmen learned that Mary McDowell was helping many Mexicans, and her fluency in two languages was a great asset. Let me tell you, those were hard times for Carmen, because she worked all day and taught English every night."

"That sounds like Carmen. But where was she living?" Amanda asked.

"She was staying with some other Mexicans in an unused train car, but after few weeks of knowing her, I asked her to move in with us. We were living in the 'back of the yards,' a neighborhood near the stockyards. My brother and I were struggling with the monthly payments, and having a third person paying helped a great deal.

"Pavel works hard. He is hoping to become a butcher, but there are a lot of men like him," Marta said in a serious way. "He says that working with the frozen beef is a lot less messy." Correctly guessing that Amanda did not know anything about the meatpacking trade, she added, "He used to work with the live stock, where the floor was covered in blood all the time. He came home from work almost unrecognizable and with a terrible smell. Ufff...I don't want to think about it," she said, pinching her nostrils as if she could smell it even now.

Amanda, not knowing what to say, just smiled.

"Look at the bridge," Marta said, pointing to an iron bridge with two strange looking towers at the ends. "This is the Halsted Lift Bridge. We are getting close." A line of cars was crossing the bridge.

"We live near the corner of Halsted and 12th Street, thanks to Carmen. She changed our lives," Marta said with a smile.

Marta continued her story, "After a couple of months of hard work on the packing line, Carmen realized that her life needed improvement. She wrote a letter to some journalist friend of hers..."

"Alma Reed. She is my friend, too, and thanks to her I found Carmen."

"Well, Alma sent a recommendation letter not only to Mary McDowell, but also to Jane Adams."

"Excuse me. Who?" Amanda felt a bit stupid, as it was clear that she was supposed to know who these important women were.

"You don't know who Jane Adams is? She is the most important woman in Chicago. She is a pacifist and the founder of the Hull House. Carmen is involved there now. Anyway, they helped Carmen get a better job working in a clothing wholesale business with offices just a few blocks from here," Marta said, pointing out the car window as if Amanda knew the geography of Chicago.

"They also gave her the opportunity to rent the new apartment where we live now, which is a big improvement over what we had."

"For her part, Carmen brought many new ideas to the Hull House. She organized activities, especially ones that were important for the Mexican immigrants. She helped to plan the Mexican street fiesta held by the Hull House and open to the entire neighborhood."

"What is this Hull House?" Amanda asked. "It sounds like a great idea."

"It's a settlement house that helps immigrants to adjust to life in America. You should come and visit it later with Carmen. It's huge, much more than a "house." There are more than ten buildings, and it has a kindergarten, art galleries, a nursery, a library, plus many activities to help the immigrants," Marta said.

The conversation stopped as Pavel pulled over to park the car. As they got out of the car, Amanda looked around. All the buildings and houses on the street were masonry, brick, and wood and seemed substantial enough, but she was surprised when Marta started taking her down an alley.

Amanda walked with Marta down the narrow alley full of garbage to the back entrance of a building. Marta opened an iron door and let herself into a small patio, across which there was another door and a window. Amanda saw the curtains of the window move and the profile of a woman behind them. Marta was already was opening the second door and calling in a loud voice, "Carmen, we are here!"

Amanda felt her heart beating fast and she rushed inside, only to see Marta standing next to another closed door, knocking to get in.

A voice came from the room, "Is Amanda there?" Amanda recognized Cacho's voice.

"Cacho, I am here! I can't believe it..." she said, while trying unsuccessfully to turn the knob of the locked door. "What is happening? Why won't you open the door?"

"Sorry, Amanda. I needed to be sure that you were not going to run inside a give me a hug. I am sick and I don't want you to get sick, too," Cacho's voice said from inside the room.

"Cacho, don't be silly. I am young and healthy. I will be fine..."

She was interrupted by the sound of strong coughing from inside the room, coughing that did not stop for almost five minutes. Amanda's impatience increased. She banged on the door and begged Cacho to open it so they could help her.

Finally, the coughing stopped and Cacho spoke again. "Not without your promise that you are not going to touch me. Amanda, you know I love you and if you love me, you will do as I ask. I have a very important task for you to do, and I need to be sure that you are going to be healthy enough to do it," Cacho said.

"All right, all right, I promise," she said. "But this is all silly." Amanda was getting nervous.

The door opened a crack. Amanda pushed it open and entered, only to see Cacho rushing across the room to sit next to the open window that looked out over the patio. Cacho's hair was so bright and black that it gave off blue tones that highlighted her face. Her face itself, however, was pale, with dark shadows under her eyes. She regarded Amanda with a broad smile and tears in her eyes. She was holding her stomach on both sides and was very pregnant.

Amanda was shocked. Cacho looked like she could give birth at any moment. Soon, however, the surprise vanished and a warm sensation of joy filled her. She ran to hug Cacho, but Cacho stopped her with a scream.

"You promised me you would stay away! I want to hug you, too, but please, don't touch me," Cacho said, holding her hands in front of her to indicate to Amanda to stay back.

"Cacho, I am so happy to see you! I have missed you so much! Since you left that night, nothing has been the same. I miss you, little sister," Amanda said with tears of joy in her eyes.

"It has been very hard for me, too, but I am happy now. Thank you so much for coming to see me. I have never stopped thinking about you, and I really wanted you to be here with me to share this incredible experience. But after the way I treated you at home, I was ashamed to ask. There are many things I want to tell you," Cacho said, stopping to cough.

After a while, she continued. "I have grown so much as a person. I have accomplished one of my life's dreams, to become an independent, responsible woman. Plus, I am helping many other women like us, like me. It is very fulfilling," Cacho said.

"Yes. Marta told me about the work that you have been doing. I am very proud, and a little envious, too."

"It hasn't been easy. The beginning was very hard, no money, no papers to prove my education, and Mexican on top of it. Many places simply refused to consider me for jobs. I looked at the big stores, but my color did not help me. Finally, I found a job on the meatpacking line, not much money, but enough. People who say that slavery has been abolished in the United States have never looked at immigrants working in the dirty jobs like meatpacking. We are paid much less than the people with papers, but at least they give us work," Cacho said.

"It was a hard life," she continued. "I had nobody. In Mexico, the family is always there to back you up. But here, there are all these immigrants who came to the United States with high hopes, only to be exploited. They spend their entire lives struggling to survive."

"I am sorry. You should have contacted us. We could have helped," Amanda said.

"The thing was that I had grown up in your house being treated almost like a member of the family, and then after that episode with the widow Peon, I blamed you. Once I got here, I saw how the world really was, and it opened my eyes. I felt ashamed of my anger and behavior toward your family. I never even said goodbye to you or your father. I felt so bad." Tears formed in her eyes.

"Cacho, we love you. You are like my sister. You don't need to be ashamed in front of us."

"I know."

"We...." Amanda did not finish her sentence. She could see that Cacho was biting her lower lip and that her face was screwed up in pain. "What's happening? Are you all right?"

"I guess this baby was just waiting for you to show up. My water broke two hours ago, and my contractions are happening every five minutes. I think..." A combination of coughs and screams came from her mouth, interrupting what she was saying.

"Oh, my God!" Marta and Amanda shouted at the same time.

"I need to get the doctor," Marta said, rushing out with a loud slam of the outside door.

"She is bringing the Hull House doctor. We talked about it earlier," Cacho said, closing her eyes once again.

"You have changed so much since the last time I saw you," Amanda said.

"I guess I dropped the lemon," Cacho said with a laugh. The closest thing they had to sex education growing up was Amanda's father telling them that the best way to avoid getting pregnant was to hold a lemon between their knees and never let it drop."

"And I made lemonade," Amanda joked. They both laughed for few minutes like they were kids again.

"I made a watermelon," Cacho said, pointing to her stomach and starting another set of laughs that mixed with coughs. "Don't make me laugh any more, or my baby is going to come out before we want him." She closed her eyes again to control the pain.

Amanda could not contain herself any longer, and gave Cacho a hug while her eyes were still closed. Cacho's eyes snapped open and she started to give a reproach, but the feeling of embracing Amanda after such a long drought was so comforting that she relaxed and let the enjoyment roll over her. They hugged each other like long-separated sisters. Cacho's breath became calmer, and Amanda felt the baby move against her. A new force was bringing them back together.

Half an hour later, the doctor arrived, full of energy. He commanded them to move the furniture in a way that positioned the bed near the window for the best light and kicked everyone out of the room.

"The fewer people, the better," he said. "The patient needs air."

Amanda and Marta left the room with worried faces. Amanda rushed to the small patio, where she could see Cacho's face through the courtyard window. She tapped on the window to catch Cacho's attention. Cacho turned, and with her finger drew a heart on the window. Amanda traced it back with her own finger.

The delivery went on for hours, but Amanda did not move from the window. A round, crying boy was born some hours later. He had rosy cheeks and a bald head. He was so busy crying that no one noticed the color of his eyes. They were gray.

The doctor forbade Cacho to breast-feed the baby; she was too weak. Marta and Amanda took on the task of taking care of him. Marta worked almost all day, so the responsibility fell mostly on Amanda. She was happy for it.

Through Hull House, Amanda found a woman who had a one-month old baby and plenty of milk to share. At first, Amanda took the baby to Hull House several times each day and brought home extra milk for the nights.

The wet nurse worked in a glove factory and was very busy, and Amanda worried about taking the baby out in the street too much, as it was beginning to get cold. Soon, Amanda looked into how much the wet nurse was earning and offered her a bit more to come to Cacho's apartment all day to feed and help with the baby. Because she could bring her own baby and spend more time with her, it was a good deal all around. This gave Amanda some free time, which she used to volunteer at the Hull House, just as Cacho had done before.

They were crowded in the small apartment. Amanda bought a bed for herself and a bassinet for the baby, and the two of them displaced Pavel from his room. All this furniture overwhelmed the room, and they needed to climb over Amanda's bed to use the door. Pavel slept in the kitchen, living room, dining room, anywhere he could find peace and quiet and a little space.

The nights were difficult. Cacho's coughing was much worse at night, and the baby woke up wanting food constantly. The situation was bad enough for Amanda, but she could not imagine having to go to work each morning as Marta and Pavel had to do.

Amanda halted all her plans. She needed to stay with Cacho and the baby. She sent a letter to the College asking for a break of one semester, but had not yet received anything in response.

Amanda and Cacho talked for hours, but continued to avoid one important topic. It was clear that Cacho was in no condition to go to Bryn Mawr, as had been Amanda's plan, nor did she want to. Amanda asked her to go back East with her and share an apartment near the school. Cacho would not give her an answer, and every time that Amanda touched the subject, Cacho changed it quickly.

Cacho's illness was worse every day. She tried to hide how sick she was, but she vomited frequently, and many mornings her sheets were sodden with sweat. The doctor visited her several times, but all he could recommend was to feed her well and be patient. Amanda cooked rich soups of chicken and beef, but Cacho was weaker and gloomier every day.

One desperate morning, Amanda painted her feet blue and walked into Cacho's room to let the light of the window illuminate her feet. She was trying to cheer Cacho up a bit, making her remember the silly game that they played as kids. In those days, Cacho and Amanda would walk to a certain part of the courtyard, and if the sun shone through a blue lead window, the girls' feet would appear blue, and they would know that it would be a good day.

Cacho looked at Amanda, appearing un-amused. After a moment, she pointed out that her feet needed to be blue as well, or only Amanda would have a good day. Amanda went for the bucket, but realized that blue-painted feet in bed would create a mess that would be impossible to clean later. Instead, Amanda ran to her room, brought back a blue dress, and hung it on the window to the courtyard. All the room was tinted blue. Cacho laughed for the first time in days. Amanda thought that she should have come up with this idea days earlier.

"Now you need to clean your feet. It will not be easy," Cacho said with a smile.

Amanda rubbed her feet with a piece of cloth, trying unsuccessfully to clean them. She groaned, and they both burst out laughing.

Every day, Amanda showed Cacho her baby through the bedside window. He was a big boy, and while sleeping looked like an angel. Cacho smiled in a melancholy way. She loved him, but her illness and weakness kept them apart.

By now, it was December, and the cold was terrible. Cacho had suffered through her worst night ever and in desperation, Amanda went to visit a doctor who specialized in tuberculosis. The doctor explained to her that there was a chance to do something. A surgical procedure could collapse the lung, giving it a chance to rest and heal. The operation was risky and expensive, but Cacho's worsening condition did not seem to offer any other chance. And Amanda was sure that her family would take care of the expense.

She returned home a little more optimistic, and hurried to tell Cacho the news. As always, Cacho was in bed. She had eaten almost nothing in the past few days, and looked even thinner than before. Cacho saw Amanda enter her room and made the familiar gesture for Amanda to sit as far from her as possible. A table between the entrance to the room and Cacho's bed formed an effective barrier. Amanda and Marta slid food across it to Cacho, and when she was finished, she slid it back. This day, as usual, the food was almost untouched. Amanda moved the table and went to sit on Cacho's bed. Cacho pulled her blanket over her head.

"I told you that I am not going to talk to you if you are near to me," Cacho said. Amanda reluctantly moved back near the door.

"All right, you win, but I want to ask you something," Amanda said.

Silence. Cacho did not respond.

"I talked to a specialist, and there is a surgical procedure that may be able to help you. I have arranged a car to pick us up this afternoon and take us to the hospital. If everything goes well, you will have the operation tomorrow afternoon." Amanda said all this in a very serious voice.

Cacho looked at her for a long time. "I am dying, Amanda, and there is nothing any hospital can do to stop it. I'm sorry."

"Cacho, please. We need to fight this. We will do it together."

"What are the chances that I am going to get better? What would they do to me in a hospital? They would cut me in half for a chance that it will be a miracle. I have a better chance to survive here in a place with people I love, where I can at least hear the distant cry of my baby in another room. Believe me, if I have any chance to get better, it will be here, with the strength of friends around me, and not in a hospital surrounded by strangers."

"Cacho, you are so frail and weak. I'm so worried," Amanda said.

"I am not worried. You are here, and you are taking care of my baby. I know that you love him as much as I do, so everything is going to be fine. I have lived through some very bad times in my life, but this is not one of them. How is Toño?"

Cacho had named the baby Antonio, but everyone called him Toño as nickname.

"He is great – sleeping through the night, as you can probably hear. His eyes are gray, and many people think that they will turn blue. He is very cute," Amanda said with a smile.

Cacho coughed for a minute, then paused and looked at the ceiling. "Do you ever wonder who his father is? You have never asked me."

"Of course I do, but I knew it was your decision to pick the right time to tell me. It's not going to change anything in how I feel toward him or you," Amanda said.

Cacho turned and look at her with an intensity that Amanda had not seen in a long time.

"If I die, you are going to take care of Toño. You should know the story. As you said, it does not matter to you, but it may matter to him. If I die, he will be your son, Amanda."

"I already love him as if he were my own son without you dying. Please concentrate on getting better, so we can all spend our lives together."

"I have been thinking about this for a long time and it has been a difficult decision. But I think you need to know the truth"

"I know that you have strong feelings about this, Cacho. Sometimes just talking about a problem with a friend can start the process of fixing it. I want to help you and can't see how this could hurt me. I am an adult, I love you, and nothing you say can change the way I feel about you."

"I'm not quite sure how to start. I guess the best way is with a fresh tortilla."

"A fresh tortilla?" Amanda asked, puzzled.

"Yes. Do you remember how we always had fresh, warm tortillas in the kitchen and how Carlos, Carlos Ancona, always went back there to snack on them?"

"Yes...."

"Well, as you know, my room was next to the kitchen, so he visited me. He visited me a lot." Cacho would not look at Amanda.

"In the beginning, we would just talk for a while because he needed to go back with you and the others, but later, he started coming to the house early so he could visit me first. We fell in love."

Cacho now glanced at Amanda, who had a blank look on her face. Amanda felt like Cacho was telling her a love story about an unknown couple. She did not feel anything.

"I felt so bad," Cacho continued. "Everyone in the house, including you, thought that Carlos was visiting because of you. A couple of times, I tried to tell you because I could see that you were starting to fall in love with him, too. It was a very difficult situation for me."

"I…"Amanda began.

"Please, let me finish. Carlos and I were in love. I felt so special with him, and loved his touch and his tenderness. My mother was very busy, so Carlos and I had plenty of time to explore our love. Those were the best times of my life, and whatever happens, I will always love Carlos and cherish those times." Cacho turned her face to the window to cover her awkward declaration of love.

"This means that Antonio is his son," Amanda said. "You know, I was not in love with him. I was in love with the idea, I was in love with the attention, but I never felt that fire inside of me toward him. It is so stupid how we make decisions when we are young. I would have married him if he had asked, but I know now that I was not in love with him."

"I am relieved to hear that, but unfortunately my story doesn't end there," Cacho said, her voice bringing Amanda back to the room in Chicago.

"He killed the Peon widow because of me," Cacho sobbed, covering her face with her hands.

Amanda could not believe that this thought had not occurred to her, but now that she had heard it, the situation finally made more sense.

Cacho continued, "He came to me right after the incident and he was furious. He went to confront the widow, but far from apologizing or offering to make amends, she called both him and me terrible names. Carlos killed her. I was in such bad shape at the time that everything is still a bit cloudy to me. But before we knew it, my brother Pedro had been charged with the crime.

"Once that happened, Carlos decided to give himself up. I was miserable. I could not stand to see him in jail because of me. I needed to do something," Cacho said, looking at Amanda and trying without success to fight another coughing attack.

When her coughing had eased, she continued, "One night, I took all the money that I had saved in my life and went to the jail, thinking I could bribe a jailer and get him out. It was the night after the assassination of Felipe Carrillo Puerto, and the jail was in chaos and half empty. None of the lead officers were in the building, and Carlos was in a cell far away from the political prisoners. I knew his general location from a cleaning lady I had bribed. I sensed an opportunity and knew that I needed to act fast."

"I had studied the layout of the jail and knew that there was an exterior door near where Carlos was staying. There were only two guards responsible for that area."

"I went to the main entrance pretending to visit an old thief who was in jail for just a few days. I guessed correctly that they had put him in the same section of the jail as Carlos. One of the guards took me there and left me with the two guards responsible for that area. As one of the guards began to walk me to the old thief's cell, I offered him all the money I had to help me with Carlos. It was a lot of money! We could live comfortably here in Chicago for a year with that amount. The guard took it, but he wanted – how can say it – more." At this point, Cacho's voice, which had already been almost a whisper, caught in her throat.

"I did what I had to do, and the guard kept his promise and opened Carlos' cell door. Carlos walked out of the prison to freedom, and, as I had hoped, found the horse that I had left ready for him. He had no idea who helped him.

"This was nine months before you arrived in Chicago to see me."

Cacho finished her story and turned to face the window. She absently traced the shape of a heart in the window, as if this shape were the seal of their secret. She did not turn to see Amanda's face, but after a time began to eat her soup between fits of coughing. Amanda was also silent. The two of them understood each other without speaking, and Amanda felt Cacho's anguish over not knowing whether Toño was part of her beloved Carlos, or some unnamed guard.

Amanda left the room when Cacho fell asleep. She scoured her face and hands, and moved to the other room where Toño slept peacefully next to the nurse.

That night, Cacho died peacefully, in silence. When they found her in the morning, the smell of vanilla filled the room.

Amanda had lost her best friend, companion, and sister, and at the same time had become a mother. As far as she was concerned, the secret of Toño's father had died with Cacho.

Amanda cried off and on for days. But while her reaction a year earlier to Cacho's beating and departure had been all-consuming, this time she faced her grief with a strange air of calm and a new maturity. It was a blessing that she had the company of Toño, who, with every scream or movement, made her feel needed and began to fill her empty places with happiness and love. She thanked Cacho for this gift of life.

One month later, she went to the county office to register the baby. She stared at the spot on the form marked "mother" and could not bring herself to write her own name. It was like erasing Cacho's memory from the Earth. In addition, the registration people wanted proof of Cacho's death and some documentation to confirm that Cacho had given the baby to Amanda before she died. Amanda left the office under the excuse that she had left the papers at home.

This marked the beginning of the lie. Amanda knew that despite the slight to Cacho, it would be better for Toño to avoid any controversy about his guardianship. Working up her determination, she went to a different registration office and registered him as her son, with father unknown. She added "Villanueva," which was Cacho's family name, as Toño's middle name, and he became Antonio Villanueva Diaz.

Would she ever tell Toño about his wonderful mother? Amanda would ask herself that same question countless times throughout the rest of her life, but kept putting off the decision.

Amanda embraced her new life with passion. Every time she changed Toño's diaper, he squeezed one of her fingers with his small hands and kicked his legs hard, ready to conquer the world.

She thought about staying in Chicago. The people she had met here were becoming a strong support network, and she had made new friends at the Hull House. As she thought about finding a college that would accept her, and knowing the demands of raising Toño, she knew she had a lot of work to do. Hull House had a nursery where she could leave the baby while she was at class, so she began to think that she and Toño could make a life in this city.

And yet, as she looked at the courtyard window and retraced Cacho's heart with her eyes, she also gazed beyond at the cold gray days and the snow-covered ground and knew that she did not belong here. The months without sun made her feel isolated, lost. And she knew that Toño had a better chance to succeed in life in her own country, where she and her family were well established.

If she returned to Merida, she would not be able to tell anyone that Toño was Cacho's son. Amanda would be seen by society as a single mother who went to the United States to cover her mistake but then changed her mind. But she did not care about society. She was sure that her family would accept them and support her, especially her father, who had always wanted a boy in the family. While Toño would grow up with a stigma attached to his parentage, at least he would be seen as part of an upper class family. Amanda would need to find a man who would love her despite her apparent faults. She remembered her time with Alberto, and found solace in the fact that such men existed.

She thought, too, of her own childhood with a ghost mother, how lonely and insecure she often felt. Moving back to Merida would give her the time to spend with Toño. Amanda's education would come to a halt, but living here and working at the Hull House had opened her eyes to social issues she could help solve in Mexico, including the rights of women and children.

She looked back at the naive girl she was just a few months ago. The few months she had spent in this place had changed her more than her entire education and life experience.

Tomorrow, she would write a letter to her parents telling them that she was coming home. Once again, she thought about a journey and the life that awaited her, but this time that life was much different from what she had expected just a few months ago. She was returning without the college degree she had craved, but inside of her was the soul of an extraordinary woman who would teach and help others.

A few days later, Amanda opened the window and a light breeze filled the room. It did not feel as cold as before. There was no fog or smoke in the air either; it was clear and refreshing, and brought Amanda's senses to alertness. She packed her things, said goodbye to Marta and Pavel, and took little Antonio home.

Chapter 11: The Final Truth

Mexico City, 1986

In the underworld of Xibalba, a beautiful princess learned of the tree in which the dark lords had hung the severed head of Hun Hunahpu, which was now sprouting flowers. As she visited the tree, Hun Hunahpu spat on her hand, impregnating her, saying at the same time:

"In my saliva I have given you my descendents. My head has no more flesh now, but so with the heads of great princes, whose flesh is only for appearance. The nature of descendents is like the saliva, they may be the sons of a lord, a wise man or an orator. They do not lose their substance when they go, but pass it on to be inherited."

- From the Popol Vuh

What events in our lives shape our personalities? Are we all born with a predisposed nature that will push us toward our fates? The events of our lives are like rain, drops of water that cover our bodies, finally becoming beautiful water marks that are absorbed through our pores to become part of us. Or they could evaporate in a moment and leave no trace.

A year had passed since my trip to Merida, and I was now on a visit to Mexico City. After following the difficult trail of Carlos Ancona, I believed I had found him.

Back in Chicago after the Merida trip, I had searched for evidence of him, finding only a few mentions of him being the son of a famous Yucatan politician and writer, Eligio Ancona.

Eligio Ancona had two boys, Antonio and Carlos, both journalists and writers. Antonio became famous. He was part of the 1912 congressional delegation that was taken to Lecumberri jail at the beginning of the Mexican Revolution, and became a hero of the Revolution. He went on to be one of the signers of the post-Revolution constitution, was a senator for Yucatan, and was governor of the territory (not yet state) of Quintana Roo, where Cancun is today. Later in life, he founded the Mexican newspaper El Nacional. He died in 1958.

A few articles mentioned Carlos Ancona, who worked for his brother both in journalism and in politics, when he was Quintana Roo's governor. Unfortunately, this period was not good to either of them.

The federal government in Mexico City sent Antonio Ancona to Quintana Roo after complaints from the landowners there that the incumbent governor was an alcoholic, partied constantly with his friends and women of questionable morals, and did nothing to execute his charge as governor. Antonio's welcome in Quintana Roo was not enthusiastic; the citizens were expecting one of their own to be appointed, and Antonio Ancona was from Yucatan. For his part, the ambitious politician Antonio Ancona felt like he had been sent to Siberia.

The chronicles of Quintana Roo are not kind to Antonio Ancona. He arrived with a woman who was not his wife, but introduced her as such to Quintana Roo society. The discovery of this lie caused an outrage. He filled the ranks of the government with people from Yucatan, and included his brother, Carlos Ancona, his cousin and even his 9-year-old nephew on the payroll. The resentment toward him was so deep that he lost the support of the federal government, and after two years, he quit and went back to Mexico City. He made peace with the politicians there and took a post as director of the civil register. He was finished with active politics.

Carlos Ancona was not as famous as his brother was, but had written a few storybooks on the legends of Yucatan that were sold in Yucatan museum stores. He became a journalist working for his brother at El Nacional, but I never found an article by him in the archives of the newspaper.

I could find no notice of his death, which I took to mean that he was still alive. I determined that my best bet for contacting him lay with the newspaper. Perhaps, he still worked there, though he would be around 90 years old by now.

I found the telephone number of El Nacional and prepared my lie. I called pretending to be a reporter wanting to interview the son of the writer Eligio Ancona, who had won a commemoration medal at the Chicago World's Fair in 1893. I claimed to be working on an article about famous Latin American journalists and writers whose descendents had become writers as well. The idea sounded a bit thin, even to me, but it was the only thing I could think of short of begging.

It worked! After my initial conversation, someone from the newspaper called back to inform me that Antonio Ancona had died, but that his brother Carlos Ancona had accepted an interview with me.

I was a family hero. I was one day away from meeting him, and I could not control my excitement. My sisters were dying to come as well. We even toyed with the idea that one of them could pose as a photographer, but we were sure that our similar looks would give us away. I knew that at some point I would likely tell him everything that we had learned, but first I wanted to hear his story. The idea that he could be our grandfather was a little crazy.

The months of searching were coming to an end. The saga that started with an old photo and a puzzling birth certificate had made our family life a constant mystery. It had been exciting, but both my sisters and I were ready to bring it to a close.

I was scheduled to meet Carlos Ancona at 11:00 in his apartment in Interlomas, a nice new neighborhood on the outskirts of Mexico City. I left Ivonne's house (where I was staying) very early, worried that I would hit the traffic for which Mexico City is infamous and be late for the important interview. I arrived an hour before the appointment and killed time in a bookstore, looking at the celebrity magazines and the books of Mexican architecture.

At exactly 11:00, I announced myself at the entrance to his building. The security people were thorough about checking my driver's license and writing the number and my name in a logbook. I waited nervously in my car while they called Carlos Ancona, and within several minutes, I was allowed inside the complex.

"Please park at the visitors' lot on the side of building A," the guard said, and I was on my way to the adventure with no turning back.

I parked my car where directed and walked to the lobby, where another guard let me know the apartment number, the right elevator bank to use, and a code that I would type into a keypad in the elevator for access to the right floor. All this security impressed me. With the crime situation in Mexico City, I guessed that this type of thing was becoming normal in buildings in well-off neighborhoods. It seemed like a good idea for an old man living alone.

When at last I knocked on the door, I looked every bit the professional reporter, with notebook ready and a small tape recorder – bought just for this occasion – in hand. A smiling older woman in a housekeeper's uniform opened the door and welcomed me into the apartment's living room. The apartment was beautiful, decorated as a rustic Mexican house, with distressed wood floors and dark brown wooden beams in the ceiling.

"He is in the office. Please follow me," the woman said. I followed her to the end of the apartment and she gestured toward the open door of the office. I entered wearing my best smile.

Bright light came through a window and it took a moment for my eyes to adjust. After a few seconds, I found myself in a room filled with books, hundreds of them, stacked on shelves and piled on the floor. Carlos Ancona sat at a desk in front of me, also smiling.

I immediately noticed his eyes. They were my father's eyes, which was funny because my grandmother always said that my father had his father's eyes, "blue as the Caribbean Sea."

He was handsome for his age. His gray hair was curly like my own, and he was dressed to perfection, with suit pants and a long sleeved shirt that looked like new.

"I apologize for not standing up to greet you properly, but my knees are not what they used to be. Please sit down. I am happy to meet you, Miss Molina."

"Thank you," I said. "It's an honor to meet you."

"'Honor' is for meeting the president," he joked. "Let's try for 'pleasure' instead. You have a Yucatecan name. Is your family from Merida?"

Here we go, I thought. I had hoped to get to this part of the conversation later, and scolded myself for not using my married name.

"Yes, my father's family is from Merida."

"Maybe I know some of your relatives. I recall having a few friends named Molina," he said, looking at me in a strange way, as if he already knew my secret and was trying to draw the truth out of me.

"Your family has been important in Yucatan for generations, hasn't it?" I asked, trying to change the subject as quickly as possible.

"Well, perhaps more 'prominent' than 'important.' As you know, my father as was Yucatan's governor, as well as a writer."

"Important enough that a medal has been named after him," I said. The "Eligio Ancona Medal" is given each year in Yucatan to people who have distinguished themselves in the arts. "Do you ever feel the pressure of being the son of someone like that?"

"Not pressure, no. It was a privilege to be his son. His name opened many doors early in my career, and I took advantage of it, as my brother did. Are you from the Molina family that owns the Clinica Londres here in Mexico City?" he asked, returning to the forbidden topic.

"No, sorry. I have found a couple of books of Mayan history that you wrote long ago, but nothing in recent years. Did you write more books with a pen name, or did you quit writing?"

"No, I can't quit writing. It is an involuntary thing for me, like breathing. I even write on the toilet paper."

I laughed.

"Finally, a laugh," he said. "You are a serious young lady. When you get to be my age, you will learn that nothing in life needs to be that serious." He laughed, too, but his expression changed into a knowing look.

"Are you related to Alberto Molina?" he asked. This time it was Carlos who was serious. I noticed the tension in his voice.

My hands trembled. I was not sure what to do, and for perhaps the first time in my life, I ran out of words. Instead of speaking, I took out the photograph from my grandmother's closet and handed it to him.

He sat in his chair with the photograph in his hand for a long time. His eyes got watery, and teardrops began to roll down his face. I had not seen many men cry like that. His tears ran fast down his wrinkled face, but behind them was a smile, a small, melancholic smile. He made no effort to dry his eyes, but turned and looked at me.

"How did you get this picture?" he asked.

"From my grandmother," I said with a shaky voice.

He smiled more broadly and asked, "Who is your grandmother?"

"Amanda Molina," I said.

"Ah, yes." He was on his feet, forgetting his bad knees. "I remember now. Amanda Diaz married Alberto Molina. And you are her granddaughter," he said, and gave me, without any reservation, a long hug.

"I could be your grandfather," he said, grasping my shoulders, holding me at arm's length and inspecting me.

"I guess you could," I said, laughing on the outside but paralyzed by inner turmoil.

He was so excited that I worried about his heart. I decided to wait to show him the other paper, the birth certificate, until after he had calmed down and I had heard his story.

"You knew my grandmother," I prompted.

"Of course I did," he said, sitting down again, but this time on a sofa facing a coffee table with a pot of tea already prepared and a plate of delicious looking cookies.

"Do you care for tea?" he asked, pointing me to a chair near the table.

"Yes, thank you." My mouth was so dry I struggled to speak the words.

"I knew all the Diaz family. They were a great bunch. I..." He paused and a shadow crossed his face.

"I visited your grandmother's house often when she was a teenager. Some of the happiest moments of my life were spent there." He looked away, hiding his expression.

"How many children did your grandmother have?" he asked after a moment.

"Two, my father and my aunt Ofelia. My father had three daughters. I am the baby."

He looked at me for a long time.

"I look like my mother's side of the family, except for this curly hair and the nose, which came from my father," I said in response to his searching look.

"Years ago," he said in a loud voice that surprised me, clearly changing the topic, "I went back to Merida. But all of your grandmother's family was gone."

"Yes. They all moved to Mexico City. My grandmother said that she could not stand to live in that climate," I said. I still wanted more information, and asked, "Have you lived many places other than Merida and Mexico City?" He might be thinking that I was a pest, asking all these questions about his background, but I was paving the way to tell him my story.

"Oh, I have been everywhere. I spent some time living in the United States and of course, when my brother was Governor of Quintana Roo, I joined him there." He paused, then added, "I am going to tell you something for your article. It concerns historical events that you may find interesting, and does not affect anyone still living."

"When Felipe Carrillo Puerto was killed, my brother went to Mexico City and blamed Calles and Obregon, the leaders of the national government, for his killing. Earlier, Antonio had personally warned Calles about the dangers in Merida and told him that Felipe needed military assistance, or at least a supply of arms."

"Calles did not appreciate that my brother was pointing fingers and telling everyone the story. You see, Felipe Carrillo Puerto, something of a martyr, was well liked at this time in Mexico City. So Calles arranged to have Antonio sent to Quintana Roo as governor, a kind of exile for him. I was just returning from the United States and he helped me to get back on my feet. Or, perhaps it is better to say that we helped each other."

"He was a bad governor. He felt that he was too far away from the real action of the government, and as a result did not pay enough attention to the affairs of the territory."

"Quintana Roo was Yucatan on a smaller scale, with its economy controlled by English and American monopolies, particularly chicle monopolies. I tried to convince him that there was much to be done to improve the lives of workers, but the truth is, my brother did nothing to improve their situation, or even that of the landowners. Facing rising unpopularity, we both left after two years and came to Mexico City. Here, he reestablished himself in the government."

By this time, Carlos once again looked calm and relaxed. I decided that it was time for my second document.

"In addition to the photograph, something else I found in my grandmother's possessions set me on this search. Before you see it, I just want to say that I am here just to learn, and you have no obligations." I handed him the birth certificate and sat back on the chair.

He took the paper. His glasses were streaked from his earlier tears, so he took them off, cleaned them, and put them on again. Finally, he looked at the paper. At first, he frowned, and I thought that he did not yet understand the mystery, but then understanding dawned on his face and once again, there were tears in his eyes.

"You are giving me quite a shock today," he said. "You are bringing alive ghosts that I thought were dead and that no one but I remembered any longer." As he spoke, he seemed to be calming down again.

"Can you tell me the story?" I asked. "Or maybe there is no story at all, and I have arrived at a roadblock in my mystery and will never know the truth."

"I will tell you the story, young lady. It is a story that has been in my heart for decades, and has been the thorn that bled it for all these years. Let me start from the beginning." He made himself more comfortable on the sofa, ready to start a long story.

"I met the Diaz family through Gualberto Carrillo Puerto, the brother of Felipe Carrillo Puerto, who was governor of Yucatan in those days. I worked for Gualberto in Merida during Felipe's administration. From the beginning, I loved the entire Diaz family. They were educated, liberal and a lot of fun. Our group of friends lounged in that house for hours at a time rather than going to restaurants and other places frequented by young people. It was a simple place where everyone could talk about anything and everything.

"It was there that I met Carmen, or Cacho, my little piece of life. She was beautiful and charming, and I loved her at once. After some time, we became lovers, but it was a hidden love. The Diaz family thought that I was visiting the house because of Amanda, and Carmen was Amanda's best friend, and a servant in the Diaz household. It was a difficult situation for us, and we were about to tell Amanda the truth when the actions of a widowed neighbor thwarted us." Carlos stopped to sip his tea. Not wanting to interrupt his train of thought, I kept silent.

"Carmen was sent to work for a widow who lived next door. Over some trivial complaint, the widow flogged her until she was unconscious. I went to see her that night and saw the horrible results on her back, plus smaller cuts on her face and hands. I went crazy, got my gun, and killed the neighbor." Carlos looked at me to see how harshly I was judging him for his actions of more than six decades ago. I just looked down.

"The police discovered the body the next day and blamed Pedro, Carmen's brother. They took him to jail. I could not bear to see an innocent man punished, so I turned myself in to the police.

"I was in jail for less than two weeks. I made friends with a guard, and one night – it turns out that it was the night after they killed Felipe Carrillo Puerto -- the guard let me out. He was a good man who was a supporter of Carrillo Puerto, and he knew that I was a friend of Felipe's. I sometimes think about that guard and hope that he did not have any trouble resulting from my escape.

"I rushed back to the Diaz house, but Carmen was gone. Her mother thought that she had gone with Pedro to the United States. She had taken all their money.

"You can imagine the frantic state of my mind. Carmen was gone and I had no way to know where she was heading, and I needed to flee as well or I would end up back in jail.

"With the little money I had, I travelled to Mexico City, where my brother hid me and gave me the money to travel to New York, where I hoped to find a trace of Carmen in the immigration records.

"I spent six months looking for her, but found no trace. I wrote to an American who was a friend of ours, Alma Reed, hoping that she might have some idea. She wrote back and gave me an address in Chicago.

"I still remember the day I took the train to Chicago. For the first time in months, I felt optimistic. I was going to marry Carmen, move back to Mexico, and have ten kids.

"I arrived in Chicago and did not hesitate a second before rushing to Carmen's address. She lived in a part of town filled with immigrants of every nationality. I knocked on her door in the middle of the day, but no one answered. I asked some kids who were playing in the alley, and they told me that two women and a man lived there, but that they worked all day. I imagined that Pedro was still taking care of Carmen, and I was happy that she was not alone in that strange city and country.

"It was a pleasant fall day, and I waited throughout the afternoon, sitting on the front steps of the various buildings around her apartment, changing places only when the tenants gave me nasty looks.

"Late in the day, I saw a beat-up car coming down the street. As it passed the place where I stood, I recognized Carmen in the passenger seat. The man driving was not Pedro, but a stranger. They parked some distance from me, and I saw Carmen being helped out of the car by a tall, blond man about 30 years old. Carmen was pregnant. She stopped to talk to one of the neighborhood kids who was playing nearby, while the man stood waiting for her at the front door of the apartment. Pregnancy suited her; she looked beautiful and elegant. She always walked in an elegant way. No one and nothing could interfere with that rhythmic, graceful walk. How I had missed her!

"After Carmen spent a moment with the kids, she and the man went into the house, closing the door on my imagination.

"My first instinct was to break down the door in a jealous rage, but despite my actions with the widow Peon, that was not my nature. Instead, I stood there, looking at a light in a window and feeling as terrible as I had ever felt in my life.

My Carmen was pregnant with another man's child, and looked to be about five months along.

"I probably would have stood there all night, but someone in the neighborhood called the police. They arrived looking quite serious, and rather than deal with them I picked up my bags (for I had come straight from the train station) and left the area. But I did not leave Chicago.

"I rented a small room in a second-class hotel not far from Carmen's apartment, and decided to follow her. I was in misery. I had no money left, having used the last of it to pay a month in advance at the hotel, and I had not written a word in months. But most of all, I had no Carmen. My love for her and jealousy over her new lover made it impossible for me to think of anything else.

"I analyzed my options. I knew that I must go to Carmen and offer to marry her and take her away from that horrible foreigner. But if she said no, the rejection would devastate me, and I was not sure I could live through it. I needed to give it my best shot, which meant waiting for the right moment. It may sound silly to you, but I felt then that I had nothing to offer to her, or at least nothing more than the foreigner with whom she was living and having a baby.

"I was a fugitive in Mexico and a nobody in the United States. Even though I spoke English well, I could not write well enough to pursue that as a career. I realized that I needed to straighten out my situation in Mexico. I wrote my brother in Mexico City a letter asking for help, hoping that there was some way to clear my name. I sent three separate letters, just in case one got lost on the way. Then, I settled into Carmen's neighborhood to wait for an answer. Meanwhile, the idea that she was intimate with him was driving me crazy. I could not believe that she had forgotten me so quickly; I knew that what we had had in Merida was unique and strong."

He paused, and I began, "Your story is very romantic..."

"Let me finish, because unfortunately my socialist thinking got me in trouble. More than that, it set the direction for my entire future.

"First, I need to give you a bit of background on the political situation in the United States at that time, so you can understand a little better."

"I am all ears," I said, settling into my chair and knowing that this conversation was likely to take some time.

"As I told you, I had settled in an immigrant neighborhood. There was a great deal of fear and resentment among the people. I met many Italian people while I was there. I liked them because we could communicate with each other using our native languages. Also, they had the same kind of large, loud families we have in Mexico. But mostly, they were fun.

"I also got to know many Russians," he added with a sad smile. "I helped the neighborhood families as a handy man, and before long they started treating me as a friend and inviting me to family get-togethers.

"The family dinners were great, but soon they started trying to match me with a cousin, a niece, or an unmarried aunt. I decided that it was easier just to visit the men, and began the custom of joining a group of Italian and Russian men who got together after work in a nearby house to have a few drinks and relax from the hard day.

"The setting was perfect for complaining and resentment. The recent years had been hard for both Italians and

Russians, and both groups had reason to be mistrustful of the American government.

"The Italians were upset because two innocent Italian men who spoke little English were in jail for murder and waiting to be executed. A known criminal who could be placed at the crime scene had confessed to the crime, but still the government refused to overturn the conviction or hold a new trial.

"Russians felt hunted and persecuted by the government because of the communist and anarchist beliefs of their countrymen back home. Things had calmed a bit by this time, but there were still many deportations from the U.S.

"To be fair, the U.S. government had reason to be suspicious of some of these immigrant groups. It is no longer well remembered, but there was a wave of terror bombings at that time, including one that killed over 30 people on Wall Street.

"The people responsible were Galleanists, followers of Luigi Galleani, an Italian anarchist who thought that violence was a good way to demonstrate against capitalism for its abuses of the working class. One of his followers in Chicago, a chef, tried to use arsenic to poison a group of wealthy citizens at a banquet.

"Most of this had happened several years before I arrived, but people in the immigrant community still talked about it all the time. Our group was only talk. We hoped for socialist improvements, but were all willing to work hard to embrace capitalism and the American dream.

"Our meetings would have gone unnoticed but for something of which we were not aware. A group of hard-core Galleanists had gone to Mexico to hide, waiting for the inevitable revolution in the U.S., and also to avoid registering for the draft."

"They thought that you were one of them," I interrupted, spellbound by his story, but no longer able to hold my words.

"Yes. The United States government thought it was suspicious that a wealthy Mexican criminal, a known socialist, was spending so much time with a group of Italian and Russian workers," Carlos said.

"They arrested us on a warm September night and I spent four months in jail, trying to explain myself. Lacking evidence of any actual crime, they deported us, me to Mexico and two others to Russia.

"While this was happening, my brother was looking into my case. The widow Peon had no family to push the case, and with several changes of the government occurring during the interim period, Antonio found that no one in authority any longer recalled that I had been jailed for that crime. Those who could recall my arrest thought it had to do with the round-up of political friends of Felipe Carrillo Puerto or that I had confessed to some crime so I could be in a better position to help Felipe."

He paused for a long moment, and as he did so, I thought about how incredible it was for me to be sitting there listening to him confessing. He was risking a great deal telling his story to a reporter, but no doubt by this time he knew the real reason for my visit.

"I ended up back in Merida, where the story made me some kind of folk hero. I was no hero. The ghost of the widow Peon haunted me. She deserved punishment for what she had done to Carmen, but I should not have killed her. I did my best to avoid the attention.

"But there I was, with no way to contact Carmen. I tried writing her, but heard nothing. Finally, I wrote another letter to Alma Reed, and she informed me that Carmen Villanueva had died of tuberculosis. I saw it as the punishment for my crime." Carlos' voice had become very low.

"I was devastated. It was then that I moved to Quintana Roo to join my brother. The first year, I struggled to open my eyes each day, but as with anything, time helped and I learned to face the rest of my life without her, but with half of my heart empty.

Carlos Ancona looked off into the distance. He was done with his story, and his body sagged from the effort of telling it.

I looked at him and had chills all over my body. At length, he looked back and we gazed at each other in silence. It felt like a tribute to his life, a silent applause.

"Did you ever find out what happened to Carmen's baby?" I finally asked.

"Don't you see? Until today, I had always thought that the father had raised him. But the dates on this birth certificate point to a child who was conceived around the last time I saw Carmen and Amanda. I knew the family well, and I am sure that Amanda was not involved with a man at that time. And Carmen's last name was Villanueva."

My mind exploded. Could this be? Carlos was saying not only that Alberto Molina was not my grandfather, but also that Amanda was not my grandmother! I had never understood the discrepancy between my father's birthday and the date on this birth certificate. Had Amanda later changed the date to make it seem more plausible that she was his mother, or to fool Alberto Molina? Was this what that friend had meant when she had told me that my grandmother had gone to the United States as a young woman and missed all the fun?

"Oh, my God," I sighed. We were both silent for a moment, trying to find the strength to continue. I said, "I don't think I want to know any more. Some things are best left alone."

Carlos Ancona stood up, took my hand, and guided me to my feet as well.

"It would be so refreshing at this time of my life to find a new family," he said. He embraced me briefly, then stepped back to look into my eyes. The intense look in his eyes made my heart want to fly out of my chest.

Had I given him false hope? Was my family's secret so much greater than I had thought when I started this quest? I looked at Carlos and his sincere, graceful smile. I might not be willing to look into this any further, but I felt that his story of love and tragedy deserved a successful conclusion.

"My father has the same color eyes as you. Eyes like the Caribbean Sea."

***

A week had passed since my eventful encounter at the apartment of Carlos Ancona. After that meeting, I went to a nearby restaurant where my impatient sisters were waiting for the news. I told them the story, to a great deal of shock and numerous exclamations, and we all agreed to take the inquiry no further. But they wanted to meet him, of course.

Carlos wanted to meet the family as well, so I set up a time when we would all get together at Ivonne's house. In honor of our native region, we had Yucatan-style food catered by a nearby restaurant called Los Almendros.

Carlos rang the bell at the appointed hour and entered bearing presents for everyone. He greeted the family in the traditional Mexican way, with a kiss on the cheek for each of the women and a manly hug with three pats on the back for my father and my husband.

For the first time, I saw Carlos and my father standing together. Although they were not physically similar, they had the same gentle look on their eyes, a soulful look combined with a smile at the happiness of life.

We had a present for Carlos, too – the hipil that Maria had given us in Merida. As he took it out of the box, he made a sound like an excited child would make.

“I recognize this dress,” he said. “Carmen worked on it for hours when she lived at the Diaz house. Many times, I saw her working on the patterns of flowers and adding new colors.” He passed his hand over the delicate flowers and rewarded us with an expression that mixed gratitude with a little light that we took as love.

The quest that had started almost two years ago had ended. The many hugs and kisses that had been missed over a lifetime would now come as an avalanche, trying to make up for lost time. I was happy to find a new person to love and a possible great-grandfather for my children, even if we would never take the steps to prove the relationship. And now, because of Carlos and the quest, I had the itch to write stories.

When it was time to eat, I noticed that Carlos was missing. I could hear him in the kitchen and walked to the doorway. From outside the room, I saw him speaking pleasantly with the catering people. He was eating a fresh, warm tortilla.

Made in the USA
Middletown, DE
30 March 2017